THE OFFERING

THE OFFERING

RUTH GATHERGOOD

The Offering

Copyright © 2019 by Ruth Gathergood. All rights reserved.

No part of this publication may be reproduced, stored in a retrieval system or transmitted in any way by any means, electronic, mechanical, photocopy, recording or otherwise without the prior permission of the author except as provided by USA copyright law.

This novel is a work of fiction. Names, descriptions, entities, and incidents included in the story are products of the author's imagination. Any resemblance to actual persons, events, and entities is entirely coincidental.

The opinions expressed by the author are not necessarily those of URLink Print and Media.

1603 Capitol Ave., Suite 310 Cheyenne, Wyoming USA 82001
1-888-980-6523 | admin@urlinkpublishing.com

URLink Print and Media is committed to excellence in the publishing industry.

Book design copyright © 2019 by URLink Print and Media. All rights reserved.

Published in the United States of America
ISBN 978-1-64367-800-9 (Paperback)
ISBN 978-1-64367-799-6 (Digital)

23.07.19

After Suzanna, Edelbert, and Father Dowling were gone, old Jimmy sneaked into the old Abbey ruin, he had been hiding behind a brumbly bush right next to the Abbey entrance, spying. The ritual had failed, and Suzanna, Edelbert, and Father Dowling had no knowledge of what happened after. The big black book had reappeared. Old Jimmy went sniffing around, he got to the alter, and right in the middle of the hexagram lay the big book. He looked around anxiously to see if there was anybody there, his heart was beating fast with fear. He then quickly grabbed the book and sneaked out very fast. The elders in the town were waiting anxiously to hear from old Jimmy, now it seemed obvious that there was more of them in the town who were members of the cult. He rushed to the village hall where they were all gathered, and much to their surprise the big black book had been found.

The village hall sat right in the middle of the village, and next to it was the library, and on the other side was the municipal offices. It had been the first building to be eracted in the village centre, and was used for various purposes.

Suzanna had arrived at auntie Doris' house who lived in Kettering, a small town some fifty miles away. Of cause she was pleased to see her and at the same time deeply saddened by what had happened to the rest of her family. All the while, one thing had been on Suzanna's mind, it was to sell Bramwell as soon as possible, and forget about everything that had happened there. And there was Edelbert as well, her plan was to get in touch with him, just to see how he was holding up. Within an hour of her arrival, she told auntie Doris of her intentions of selling Bramwell. With all good intentions auntie Doris prompted her to go ahead and waste no time.

Back at the village hall, old Jimmy arrived with the book, and then he handed it over to Roger Simms the head elder. Being a Saturday, the cult members gathered in the village hall as it was their weekly routine to run meetings there or rituals they deemed necessary, besides days of the full moon where they worshipped their moon goddess represented by a serpent. On a full moon day they bring in a green serpent that they would dance around while singing and making chants, this was to gather the strength of the serpent goddess. Sexual rituals also happened there, where they initiated a virgin girl and a virgin boy. They believed that the mating of the two in front of the crowd brought fertilty, good health, and long life. None of them knew of what had happened at the Abbey only a few hours before.

Old Jimmy entered while heaving away with both fear and excitement. He interrupted the meeting, then pulled Roger Simms to the side and explained what he had witnessed. He had been spying at the Abbey and had watched the whole exorcism ritual which father Francis had attempted and failed. He knelt down and handed the book over to Roger. Roger touched his shoulder as if giving blessing to Jimmy, he took a sigh and said, "This is the book I have been waiting for all my life." He rubbed the book gently and smiled, it was a smile of accomplishment. "Well done old Jimmy, I knew I could put my trust in you," he said as he pulled old Jimmie's ear playfully. "Well done," he repeated. "You can get up, and go join the others, and don't tell anyone at all what you have just told me. Go!" he insisted. Old Jimmy got up, "Thank you sir," he replied, then he went to join the others as he was told. He felt uncomfortable and kept looking around at the other members of the cult with a bit of suspicion. Roger stood still for a while, and kept admiring the big book and rubbing it gently. He shook his head then swung his long robe around and headed to some secret place where he locked the book away. His robes were red in colour with a hoodie attached to it. It was only the top order of the elders who wore the red robes, the rest wore black with hoodies attached as well. Roger joined the rest and acted normal, he was reserving revealing what had happened at the abbey for another time after he had done some digging. The meeting went as usual and before long time passed and they all dispersed.

In Kettering Suzannna found an agent willing to sell Bramwell, the ball was rolling and she felt a sense of relief, and so did auntie Doris. Days that passed, Dr Edelbert quickly adjusted back to his old routine of hospital work, and Suzanna soon found a buyer for Bramwell cottage. As for Father Dowling he had simply vanished, Roger had even send a search party to find him but to no avail. After the failure of the exorcism, he feared for his life from the village cult members, he left that village that very same day without leaving a forwarding address, he had simply vanished into thin air. Carlos and Audrey's children soon learnt about what had happened to their parents, it was bitter sweet news of cause, but the cult issues was no surprise to them at all, they were fully aware of their parents involvement and the possible consequences of belonging into something like that. None of their children mourned for them. Their oldest son decided to move into their cottage, him joined by his wife and two kids. There had been talk before that, any villager threatening to expose the cult to the outside world would be ousted and terrorised by the community, even be killed. Carlos and Audrey's son Justin and his wife Aida and their two sons, Trevor and Charles soon moved into their new home which was next to Bramwell. The villagers gave them a warm welcoming, and soon they were settled in. Trevor and Charles got into jobs at the local municipality doing some clerk work. Justin was a handy man doing odd jobs, and work was coming flying in for him, and Aida was a mere housewife, so they were doing okay for money.

Soon Bramwell was occupied as well, by the Lawrence family, it was a family of a mother and a father and three children, two boys and a girl. The boys Tobin and Robert were twenty one year old twins, and Rebecca who was twenty three. Mr Lawrence whose first name was John, was a post master who had moved into Bramwell because of a job offer, he was going to be the new post master of the village, his wife Rosie was a housewife just like Aida. Rebecca was looking for work, all she had known was to work in grocery stores, while the twins were in apprenticeships. The twins enrolled themselves in the local college to persue with their courses, and of cause Rebecca was hunting for any job really.

Chapter 1

The Lawrences were out dining at the Hilsbury restaurant in the village, it was a way for them to get to know the village and meet other villagers. It was the most popular restaurant constantly full of people. Roger and his family happened to be dining there as well, so he came to introduce himself, and he introduced other local villagers who were dining there. "How pleasant they all seem," remarked Mr Lawrence to his family who by then had moved on to having their desserts. "They seem nice," replied his wife. It wasn't long after that remark that the restaurant grew quiet, it became uncomfortable. Soon enough everybody in the restaurant was staring at theLawrence family that they picked up on it, and had to leave straight away before finishing their dessert. "I take it back," said Mr Lawrence, "they are not nice people at all. There is more to them than they appear, perhaps there is something dark and sinister about them, more like a conspiracy going on here," he added while shaking his head in disbelief." How quickly moods can change, was it to save some purpose, or was it merely coinscidence. Mr Lawrence, without wasting time ushured his family out of the restaurant, he didn't even bother tipping the waitress before leaving. It appeared rude for the man at the desk, but given the circumstances, Mr Lawrence felt he was part of the perfomance, very much involved; so he didn't feel bad at all. "What have we gotten ourselves into, this could end up being a nightmare. It is never too late to turn back to the city you know!" he insisted to his family, he panted as he led the way out of the restaurant. "I don't understand why you are brooding," replied Mrs Lawrence. "I guess you are reading too much into things, as you always do John," she panted. Tobin, Robert, and Rebecca remained quiet, none of them was in a mood for an arguement, so they left their parents to it. After all they were already missing their friends, and the life they had in the city, it was too stressful for them to even bother. They sat in the car in silence as they drove back to Bramwell. None of them thought of anything, it was pure bliss for them not to participate in petty arguements. When they got home, it was late, and they were all exhausted except John who remained restless. He was afraid, all of a sudden he felt a cold chill running through his body. "I don't like this feeling I am having," he told his wife. "I feel afraid, call it gut instinct," he hesitated. "I have got a strange feeling about this place, I feel something evil is lurking around us," he continued as he lay in bed staring at the ceiling. "I can't sleep," he perpetuated. "Why?" replied Rosie. She turned her back to face her husband who was looking lost in space, more bewildered than anything else. The boys and Rebecca were heavily sedated with exhaustation falling asleep came easy for them. Soon after midnight they were all woken up by loud bangings on the front door. The knocks were so loud that they couldn't be ignored. The banging carried on that John jumped out of bed, got a baseball bat which once belonged to one of the boys, he went downstairs to answer the door. His eyes were looking bloodshot with exhaustion, he barely made it to the door. "Who is there!" he yelled when he got to the door. "I have got a gun," he shouted before he opened the door with anticipation. There was noone outside, "I have got a gun! you might as well show yourself!" he shouted. There was no reply, he wallked round the house to see if there was anybody there, but still nobody showed up. "I must be losing my mind," he whispered to himself before getting back in the house. He locked the front door, double checked to see if it was locked, then he bolted the door. As soon as he turned round to make his way back upstairs, he heard the loud knock again. "Who is it?" he yelled again. "Let me in father," a voice replied. It was a voice of a young woman. "Who are you?" he responded. There was a moments silent, then the voice replied, "Let me in father, I am afraid," It was a mourning desperate voice. John opened the door again, but there was nobody there. He shook his head, "I must be dreaming," he said to himself then went back upstairs. He opened Rebecca's door to check if she was in, if she wasn't in, perhaps it was her locked outside,' he thought. But Rebecca was sound asleep in her bed, so it couldn't have been her. He shut her door gently then went to bed. He couldn't sleep, he kept thinking about what might be going on, perhaps he was losing his mind after all. His wife slept soundly. Two hours passed, he still couldn't sleep, all of a sudden there was bangings on the walls, the noise woke the whole family up including Rebecca who was always a sound sleeper. "What is that racket!" shouted Rosie. She got up, and put her dressing gown on, by then John was in the hallway holding his baseball bat, ready to strike at anything. "I don't know!" replied John. Their kids were up as well, and they all gathered in the hallway. Rebecca was shaking, and started crying, being the weakest one of them all, she hid behind her mother. "Is this place haunted or what," she cried. "What is happening here dad?" questioned Tobin. "Earlier someone was knocking on the door, and when I went out there, there was noone. I heard a girl calling out, but there was noone there," whispered John. The bangings on the walls perpetuated, and the floors were squicking. The noises became so loud that it was deafening, they all covered their ears. "Let's get out of this house now!" yelled John. They ran outside, John grabbed the car keys from the kitchen cabinet, and eventually they found solace in the car as it was a bitterly cold night to be outside. They sat in the car patiently, and before long Rosie and Rebecca had nodded off to sleep. John and the boys were discussing on what to do next. "We can't go knock on our neighbours because it is very late," said John. "You are right there John, maybe we can go there in the morning," replied Rosie as she awakened, and had barely heard John. They sat in the car contemplating for a good couple of hours wondering what to do. "Maybe the noises have subsided, perhaps we should go back in the house," declared John. "Not a bad idea," responded one of the boys. They decided to go back in, to their surprise the noises were gone. "Something doesn't want us in this house," ejaculated Rebecca. "Uuh! something spooky hey," laughed Robert. "Maybe we need an exorcist, how adventurous that would be," he mocked. Tobin kicked Robert in a joking manner, then remarked, "That should make a good newspaper story. I have always wanted to be in journalism," he jeered. They both laughed. After that talk, there was dead silence,

John and Rosie went to bed, and soon the rest followed suite. They slept soundly without any further disturbances.

The morning was blazing with sunshine, the Lawrences were up bright and early, and were happy to greet the new day with optimism. Breakfast was extraordinarily early as John had to be out early for work, the boys start was a lot later than their father's. None of them spoke of the happenings of the night before, and before long it was just Rebecca and Rosie left in the house. "Call me if anything happens," said John to his wife, "and take extra care, keep the doors locked, and don't let anyone in the house," he added before he left for work. Rosie and Rebecca cleared the dishes, and afterwards they had a lot of work to do, unpacking all them boxes in the house. Rosie went to the kitchen to unpack the rest of the boxes with kitchen utensils. She stood by the window, then she saw some old lady in the chicken coop, she appeared to be feeding the chickens. The chicken coop was right at the bottom of the garden, but visible from the kitchen window. "Rebecca come quick!" shouted Rosie, "there is someone in our garden!" Rebecca dropped what she was doing, then ran downstairs. They stared at the old lady, and Rosie decided to go talk to her. "Stay indoors and lock the door," she said to Rebecca before going to the coop. It was Ms Biggs, after the tragedy that happened to Susanna's family Bramwell stood empty, and Ms Biggs used to come round to feed the chickens that were left there, she thought the cottage was still empty. "I'm Ms Biggs," she said smiling away, "I have been coming here to feed the chickens otherwise they would have starved to death. I didn't know anybody had moved in," she grinned. "I am Rosie the new owner," Rosie replied. They shook hands. "So what brought you here?" Ms Biggs asked. "My husband's work," Rosie replied. They chatted for ages, till Rosie invited her in the house. Rosie introduced her to Rebecca, and they sat in the kitchen drinking tea and chatting away. "I am a nosey old lady, that's what it is, and often it has led me into a lot of trouble around here," she said. "Don't trust anyone around here, I am warning you," she urged. "There is something evil here, and everyone is on it. Soon enough you will find out," she cooed. She fiddled with her hands in an uncontrollable manner, she grew nervous. "What are you talking about?" asked Rosie in a concerned manner. Rebecca looked at her mum in a worried manner. She was suspicious of Ms Biggs, she winked at her mother as if to warn her not to trust Ms Biggs. "What do you mean by that Ms Biggs?" she asked again. Ms Biggs sipped her tea, she regained her momentum and began, "This cottage has got a history, so many tragedies happened in this house, some believe it is associated with some satanic cult. The history began even way before I was born," urged Ms Biggs. "I can't tell you anymore otherwise I will get myself in trouble, it's no use for me being here, I have got to go! I have got to go now!" she insisted. "You see, I have done it again! I am a stupid old lady! I should learn to mind my own business! this time they are going to kill me!" she exclaimed. "Who is going to kill you Ms Biggs?" questioned Rosie. Ms Biggs galloped down the remaining of her tea, then she got up racing for the front door. "Wait Ms Biggs," cried Rosie, "where can I reach you?" she asked. Ms Biggs by then was by the door, "I live at the house right on the corner of Baldon road near the creek, and opposite Almer primary school. It is the house with a red front door, you can't miss it," she replied. She dashed out and left. Rosie and Rebecca were left in awe. "None of us knew before we moved here, that there was some chickens at the bottom of the garden," remarked Rebecca. "There must have belonged to the family who lived here before us, and why didn't they take them with them when they left?" queried Rosie. "I guess that is what Ms Biggs was trying to tell us, that a tragedy happened to them, they didn't leave, they perished here" she exhausted. "This is scary mum," exclaimed Rebecca. "It wouldn't hurt getting acquinted to the neighbours, they must know something," added Rebecca. Rosie was washing up the dishes as they spoke, "Mmmm," she murmmered, "perhaps we should invite them for dinner, with your father's permission of cause," she cooed. Rebecca picked up from where she left unpacking the kitchen boxes, she was absent minded still thinking about what Ms Biggs had told them. "Dad will never allow that, he is half suspicious of the people around here already, surely he doesn't want us to have anything to do with any one of them. He is going to hit the roof if he learns that we allowed Ms Biggs in," she perpetuated. "Do you think there is any truth in what Ms Biggs said?" asked Rebecca. "I guess we have to find that out ourselves," she continued. "I am open to believing anything," replied Rosie. "She is a funny lady anyway, maybe there is something mentally wrong with her, but I guess we will find out in time," continued Rosie. "Don't you think those people were a bit funny in the restaurant, that is what made dad suspicious of them," Rebecca responded. "They were pretty odd, perhaps that's the way they do things here, I am sure time will reveal all," exclaimed Rosie. They carried on unpacking till all the boxes were empty, they put the house in order, and went on to cleaning. They polished all the floors, scrubbed the bathrooms, and cleaned the windows of the whole cottage. There was still work to do, they had to clean off all the cob webs which had semi taken over the cottage, and besides they had to get rid of some of the old furniture which had been left in the cottage by the previous occupants. They didn't need that furniture, it was crowding the cottage, so between the two of them they moved the furniture out into the storage room which was situated in the bottom of the garden. The storage room was quite large, roughly twenty by twenty feet in size, and it was near empty with just a couple of chest of drawers and a desk. Rebecca tried opening the drawers of the desk, but they were locked, as for the chest of drawers, there was nothing inside of them. Rosie and Rebecca filled the storage room with all the unwanted furniture from the cottage till they could barely shut the door, it didn't matter much to them as they were never going to need anything from there, as far as they were concerned the storeroom had served its purpose. Time had moved so fast, that before they knew it, John was back from work and the boys from college, nothing extra ordinary had happened to them while they were away. Rosie and Rebecca decided not to say anything at all about Ms Biggs. "I see you have been busy, all boxes seem unpacked," said John to Rosie. "Yeh! what a day it has been, but everything will be alright," replied Rosie, she felt hesitant. "Work has been fine, everybody has been nice. I don't know what I was thinking, having horrible thoughts about these people. Infact they are the loveliest people I have ever met," said John in an excitable manner. "It's the same for me mum," responded Tobin, "I had a great day too, I believe that, we pre-judged them.

The Offering

How was your day Robert?" asked Tobin in a seemingly positive manner. "You had a great day too, didn't you," he continued in a patronising manner, as if bullying Robert into submission. "My day was good, no problems whatsoever," replied Robert. He started scratching his head, and he was matching up and down as if he was unsure of himself. "I agree, that what we thought, or felt about this community is absurd. He shook his head and asked, "When is supper mum," he was unsure of himself. The reality of it was, he didn't have a good day, he was bullied, patronised and trodden on by the other students that he wanted to leave in the middle of lessons, but however he chose to stick it out. "I am tired and hungry mum, so I am going to take a nap in my room, wake me up when dinner is ready," he said. He matched to his room, the truth is that, college on that day exhausted him, the amount of bullying, patronization left him exhausted and desperate to quit, just for that day. Rosie and Rebecca remained quiet about Ms Biggs, they went on to prepare dinner, and everybody was fed well, without a complaint. None of them spoke much for the rest of the evening till they all retired to bed. As they slept soundly in their respective beds, Rebecca was woken up by noises coming from her bedroom. She heard the voice of some old woman whispering in her ear, "Get out of this house now," the voice whispered. She woke up in fright, she listened attentively, the voice spoke again, "Get out of this house immediately, it's not your house, it belongs to us," the voice whispered again. Rebecca didn't know what to do, she ignored the voice, and went back to sleep. It wasn't long after she fell asleep than she was woken up again, she heard foot steps walking up and down the stairs. The foot steps were varied, one minute it would be heavy footsteps, and the next light foot steps as if pitter pattering up and down the stairs. The noise became so loud that the family was woken up again, John being the man of the house took control inorder to protect his family from whatever it was that was threatening them. The minute they were up, the foot steps stopped. He went downstairs to check the whole house. He got to the lounge, there was noone there, but the fire was on, none of them had put the fire on, then he went to the kitchen, the taps were on, and the water was dripping onto the kitchen floor, somehow the sink plug was on and caused the overflow of the water. "What is this?" he asked himself. He called out to Rosie, "The rest of you go back to bed!" he shouted. The kids did what they were told, so they went back to bed, and Rosie went downstairs to assist John with whatever was happening downstairs. When John told Rosie about the fire, and the kitchen taps, Rosie decided to tell him about Ms Biggs visit and what she had told her. John couldn't make any sense of it, he called it a lot of rubbish. "I told you not to let anyone in the house!" he yelled. "For all you know, she could be the one causing all this," he replied in a furious manner. "Well you better clean up this mess in the kitchen, and as for the fire we will leave it burning till it burns out," he added. Rosie went on to mop the kitchen floor while John went outside with a torch to see if there was any intruders lurking about, but there was nobody there. They went back to bed and there was no further disturbances throughout the night.

Chapter 2

John was stocky in built, about six foot tall, broad shouldered, and always wore a crooked smile. His sharp nose, and blonde hair and narrowed green eyes made him appear like a shrewd man, and rather too serious in nature. His shrewd and serious manner was so rigid that noone could get threw to him. Tobin was a lot like his father, stocky, broad shouldered and green eyed, the only difference was that he was slightly shorter than John, and very different in character. Toby, as they called him in short, had a habit of biting his nails when confronted by a problem, he would avert problems if he could, and choose to be reclusive if possible. He was an ambitious young man that settling for something like a clerk's job was a big no no to him. He wanted to fly high in terms of career and development. If confronted with problems, often he would be agressive inorder to avoid the given issues. On the other hand Robert was the complete opposite of the two, he was a lot more outgoing, always bubbly in nature, he never took life seriously, many a time when confronted by issues that need instant attention, he took to a careless attitude, it made him happy. He had to protect that strength of his which kept him in a perpetual happy mood. "We should have named you Joy," his mother often said when she was in a happy mood, of which was rare. Rosie was a focused woman who had brought her kids up with values and a sense of stracture. Amidst crowds, or in any social occassions, her kids never spoke to the elders unless spoken to. They had such good eticasy and table manners, all thanks to Rosie. She was short in stature no more that five feet tall, dark haired with grey receedings in the front of her hair. She was a cautious woman, always ready to do anything for her family, to ensure their safety. She was rather plump, and her face was plump too, with red cheeks that seemed tatooed on her face. It was hard to read expression off her face as she wore the same expression permantly, an unsure grin, raised eyebrows, and a glinter in her light brown eyes. She suffered from constant back pain. Some say chronic illnesses are a result of constant worry, it seemed to be the case with her. She often dyed her hair to cover the the grey receedings. She had plump pudding fingers, and toes, often when alone in the house, she enjoyed comfort eating, mainly cakes and biscuits, that is why she could never shed the weight. Often she would stuff her face with biscuits and cakes, even while she was making dinner for the family. Her hair was curly, but she often went to the hairdressers at least twice a week to have it straightened out, if she didn't make it to the hairdressers her hair would be so curly that you would easily mistake her for a hobbit. Rebecca was her complete opposite they looked nothing alike, she was tall and slender, had a beautiful face, she was more or less delicate, with big green eyes that were mesmerizing, she had long dark hair, and a smallish nose, and a few freckles on either side of her cheeks. Rebecca was somewhat an enigma, often kept herself to herself. She was highly sensitive in which came about from being bullied terribly in high school, the feelings of that were still raw inside of her, it made her suspiciuos of people and insecure. However she battled with the feelings quite well, under no circumstances did it make her disfunctional. She was a fighter and a survivor. She didn't do well in social occassions, she would often hide behind Rosie. She was extremely loyal to her family that often her brothers relied on her ambuguity. Rebecca often dismmised problems, she would rather be in denial than confront a problem. Their conflicting personalities often caused regular arguements within the family.

Days that came Rosie kept talking about their neighbours, and how lovely it would be for the family to get to meet them. One day Rosie took it upon herself to invite the neighbours for dinner, John mumbled in agreement just to get Rosie off his back. They knew that the neighbours was a family of four, a couple and their two boys. The boys were in their twenties.

It took a lot of preparations from Rosie; as a perfectionist everything had to be right, she roasted a couple of guinea fowls, roasted some parsnips and potatoes, boiled peas and broccoli. For dessert she baked an apple pie which she was going to serve with home made custard. She was a skilled cook, I guess it came from her taking a short cookery course just before the family moved to Bramwell. The Menderaz family arrived on time as expected seven o'clock evening. They were very well dressed, Justin, Trevor, and Charles were dressed in suits, and wore shiny black shoes. As for Aida, she wore a navy blue costume that comprised of a straight skirt and a jacket with pumped up sleeves, and a white blouse with frills for a collar. She wore black shoes that she could barely walk in because they were high stiletoes. For her it was all about making an impression. John who was normally grumpy to strangers was very warm, he greeted them with open arms, and was very chatty. He led them to the dining room which was nicely decorated, and the table looked beautiful because Rosie had gone an extra mile to make it a candle light dinner. She had spend a good part of the afternoon polishing her cutlery. The candles were scented, giving off an unmistakeble smell of lavender. By the time the Menderaz's arrived everything was more or less ready, the guinea fowls had been roasted and were resting, potatoes and everything else was pretty cooked, it was just the serving left to do.. Rebecca helped her mother with the dishing of the food, while Robert and Tobin entertained the Menderaz boys. They shared their experiences, and even talked about paranormal activities, how ever they did not speak about the experiences they had at Bramwell, John would never have allowed it. John had to carve the birds while Rebecca and Rosie served.

Justin was a man in his late fiftees, and his wife Aida was a couple of years younger than him, their twin boys were twenty three years old. They were not identical twins and had totally diferent personalities. Trevor was rather shy, while Charles was the exact opposite, more outgoing and flamboyant. He always yearned to having a good time in whatever he did, and wherever he went, so convesartion was flying everywhere throughout the evening. Justin spoke briefly about his parents, Carlos and Audrey, and how sweet they were. He chose not to speak about their deaths, but however he spoke fondly about his childhood growing up in the cottage. "We only moved here a few days before you," he said grinning away.

"Infact our cottage go a long way before, it was my great grandfather who bought the cottage, and after that it has remained in the family," he said proudly. "It is what you call an heirloom, we are proud of our heritage," he boasted. He fiddled a bit in his chair, coughed a little then preceeded, "My father was well known member of the community, so it hasn't taken us long to get aqueinted with the community. Everybody here knows who we are," he boasted some more. "We are part of the brickhouse, as they say. We are the brick that makes the house complete," he exhauled. "How well do you know this community? because we have had some weird reception, and have experienced weird phenomenas in this house," said John. He was playing uncomfortably with his cutlery, and often finding himself shaking his head with suspicion, as the conversation carried on. There was a brief silence at the table, they were all looking at each other in a funny way. Justin nodded his head as he munched uncontrollably into the guinea fowl's leg, he put the cutlery aside and he was using his hands to devour the leg of the fowl. It was so greasy that you could see the fat dripping down onto the sides of his cheeks, he was over excited. He poured some more red wine into his goblet, and gobbled it down. The goblets was one of the few things the Lawrences had found in the kitchen cabinets when they moved in, but they were going to put them to good use especially on an occassion like this. He was a greedy man anyway, he could have easily sucked through the fowl's bones till the marrow was no more. "I trust them fully, I mean the people round here. They have got such a strong community spirit, and loyalty on top of that. I urge you to trust them, put your whole trust in them, then you will see for yourselves," he urged as he took another mouthful of his roast potatoes and broccoli. "We saw you at the restaurant," blutted Trevor. "What were you doing there?" he asked in a perplexed manner. "Oh! it was nothing," swallowed Rosie, "we just wanted to get acquainted with the community," Rosie was smelling a dead rat. "How is your dinner?" she asked trying to change the subject. "It's great thank you," the Menderaz family replied simuteneously. There was a stiff silence after that, all you could hear was cutlery in motion. Rosie then went on to serve the apple pie and custard. Justin was over ready for his dessert,

"Is this apple pie home made?" he asked as if he were an excited little boy ready for some treat. "Yes it is, Rebecca and I made it together. You see, she often helps me in the kitchen preparing dinner. What a blessing it is," she smiled. They all looked at Rebecca, and praised her for her efforts. "What a wonderful spread," added Justin, "we should come here more often." He took a sigh, as if it were for digesting his dinner. "We would like to return the favour, infact we are inviting you to our house for a barbecue this Saturday afternoon, please say yes," he pleaded. It was only two days away before their barbecue, John needed a bit more time to think about it before making a commitment. "I need to think about it," he replied, "I have to look at what plans we have for the weekend," he smiled at Justin. Rosie was playing with her hair as she often did when faced with a predicament, "Saturday will be fine! we will be there," she blurted out. She wanted to find out more about the Menderaz's and the rest of the community, what could be better opportunity to know them better and the rest of the community. She didn't care about what John thought, after all he always did what she said. After they had their apple pie, John's kids disappeared from the table with the Menderaz's boys, they went to the lounge; if the adults wanted a place to disappear as well, there was always the drawing room, but they chose to stay in the dining room, induldging themselves with bottles of red wine. The lounge was a big room possibly twenty feet by twenty feet, the furniture made it very cozy, alongside the blazing fire. There was an old piano in one corner, since none of John's family were able to play, most likely the piano belonged to the previous occupants. In the lounge Rebecca started talking about the weird nights that they had experienced at Bramwell, she told the Menderaz's boys about Ms Biggs, and what she had told her and her mother about the phenomenas of Bramwell. "We heard that Ms Biggs is a nut job, that she is crazy, dillusional and psychotic. We were warned by the community here to ignore her," exclaimed Trevor. "Don't listen to a word she says!" warned Charles, "Father says the Mayor warned him not to have anything to do with her, because she is a trouble maker," he urged. Tobin and Robert looked at Rebecca in a stern manner, "how come you didn't tell us before about Ms Biggs?"

enquired Robert. "Rebecca felt uncomfortable, "well," she replied, "because mom told me not tell anyone about it. You know how dad is cautious about people, he would go mad, if he realizes that we let her in the house." "I don't mean to be funny or anything, my mom once told us about some tales about your cottage that it was haunted and affiliated with some sort of cult. It was probably nothing of cause," said Trevor. "Yeh, I think it was nothing as well," interjected Charles. "Strange things have been happening here since we moved in," said Rebecca. She was a naturally suspicious person, John had told the kids not to talk to anybody about the strange happenings, but there was Rebecca spilling the beans, she wanted answers. Tobin and Robert didn't speak about it, they were silent as Rebecca spoke. "We have been hearing bangings on the walls at night and footsteps everywhere while we slept; there was also knockings on the door and noone there. This place is definately haunted," she nodded. As she spoke she was becoming more and more nervous and agitated. Robert and Tobin kept looking at each other nervously as Rebecca spoke. "Let's change the subject, enough of this hocus pocus," intervened Tobin, he could see that his sister was getting worked up. Instead the Menderaz boys spoke about their jobs, and places of interest they had discovered in the village. At the end of the night the Menderaz's boys were looking forward to seeing Tobin, Robert and Rebecca at the barbecue that Saturday. Trevor had taken a liking to Rebecca, his thoughts were, he wanted to know her better. John also had taken a liking to Justin and his wife, and it was the same for Rosie who thought they were a nice couple. The evening went well, by the end of the night the Lawrences were tired and were looking forward to a good nights sleep. Rosie had a habit of never going to bed until all the dishes were washed and put back in the respective kitchen cupboards, so she and Rebecca cleared the kitchen and the rest of the house, and the Menderaz's were gone. It wasn't long in the night, that the disturbances started again, there was a pattern to the noises, they always started after midnight. It started in Rebecca's room, she was woken up to hearing a girl's voice singing. The voice was so soft that it could easily been a lulla-by, she woke up. After the singing voice, was whispering things that she couldn't understand. Rebecca chose to ignore, and buried her head under the bed covers. The voice then changed to whinning, 'help me dad! help me dad!' the voice whimpered. The voice went from whimpering to screaming for help, that is when she couldn't ignore anymore. She was startled, she sat upright in bed scared, then she heard the footsteps marching up and down the stairs. The foot steps stopped by her door, she was silent, and didn't move at all, she held on to her covers tightly until she heard the footsteps walk down the stairs. She saw a figuren of a young woman, young and beautiful standing by the fire place in her room. "Help me! I am trapped, and I don't know where I am!" the young lady said before she disappeared into thin air. Immediately Rebecca pulled the covers over her head, she was scared. The bangings on the walls and the front door started again that the whole family was woken up. John and Rosie were up followed by Tobin and Robert, the noises were outrageously loud that Rebecca being highly sensitive covered her ears with the pillow. John went downstairs to check the house, and outside where he didn't find anybody there. Rosie followed behind, "What is happening here?" she asked John; "I think this house is haunted," she cried. Rosie started crying, holding John's hand, she sobbed and sobbed till she owned up again to John about Ms Biggs' visit, and what she had told her and Rebecca. His responses were non surprising than before, he told Rosie off for allowing a stranger in the house. "She is probably the one behind all this," exclaimed John. "You don't even know this woman! and you let her in our house! gees Rosie! what were you thinking! You saw how this community reacted towards us in the restaurant, and you let her in! Are you mad!" he shouted. He calmed down, then said, "We don't know any of these people well enough, so please Rosie try to understand where I am coming from. It's one thing being polite, and it's another thing being nai've enough to endanger the family," he exhaled. "But I didn't endanger anybody, I was just trying to get to know them. Take Ms Biggs for example, we can actually learn something from her about this community," she expressed. "Perhaps what she said has got relevance to the horrible experiences we are having here," she added. John shook his head, "it's a bunch of mambo jumbo, if you ask me," he responded as he walked away from Rosie into the drawing room. The fire was ablaze and yet John remembered putting it out before he went to bed. He was starting to believe Rosie about the cottage being haunted. The bangings carried on, Tobin and Robert who were downstairs as well, were in shock; Rebecca decided to join them too. Robert went to the kitchen where his mother was, she was literally shaking with fear; he comforted her by putting his arm around her. "It's going to be alright mum," he said as she buried her head in his arms. "Why don't you go sit down in the drawing room, I will get you a hot drink" he said. Tobin was the least worried of them all, "If there is ghosts in this house, rest assured, they are harmless, they could have hurt us by now if they were dangerous," he said to his family who by then were gathered in the drawing room. Rosie was still shaking sitting by the fire, and Rebecca was next to her with her blanket. Perhaps we should call an exorcist or some priest," said Rosie. Robert was sat opposite his father, thinking away, he replied, "Don't be hasty mum, we need to find out more, before we can start delging into things we do not understand," he expressed. "I am going to look round the house to check if there is somebody out there, it could be some people playing tricks with us." He got a torch, "Be careful out there," urged Rosie, "go with your brother," she cried. Tobin shrugged his shoulders, "I am not going out there," he said. "You chicken shit, I will go by myself," responded Robert. Tobin began biting his nails as a sign of his insecurity, he would rather curl up in a ball than confront whatever it was out there haunting his family. Robert walked out, he started with checking the front garden, there was nothing out there, then he opened the side gate and went round the back garden. As he walked past the chicken coop, and past the storage room, he saw something. His torch was giving limited visibility, but he saw something right at the end of the garden, he saw multiple torches, not electric torches but fire torches, quite a few of them. As he approached closer, he saw about ten people holding torches, they were dressed in hoodies performing something that resembled a ritual. They were formed in a circle, then afterwards were dancing around the circle. He kept his distance because he didn't want his presense to be known. He was literally tip toeing closer and closer, he saw the people dressed in black robes, he couldn't differentiate whether they were men or women, or both. As he got closer, he saw a man right in the centre of the circle, his robe was different from the rest, his was red in colour, presumably the leader of the cult. They were chanting and dancing round the circle. Robert hid behind a birch tree which was a couple of yards away from them, he remained silent as he watched what was going on. He heard the sound of a baby crying. One of the members was carrying a baby and handed the baby over to the leader who was in red robes. Robert remained watching without making a sound. The leader drew a big knife from his pocket, and slushed the baby's throat while they all watched, and chanting some words that he couldn't understand. The one who carried the baby forward, drew a chalice from his pocket, chanted something, then started collecting the baby's blood into the chalice. The leader then drank from the chalice and handed it back to the person who handed the baby, he drank from it before passing it to the rest of them, who then drank from it. They stopped the dancing and the leader spoke a few words as he held the dead baby up, as if to complete the ritual. Robert kept watching, till after a little while they all disappeared into thin air. He started questioning his reality, did he imagine all of this? or was it real, he started questioning himself. He ran back into the house heaving with fear. "Well did you find anything! hero!" questioned Tobin in a sarcastic voice. Robert was still breathing heavily, he couldn't believe what he had just witnessed. "Well! ain't you gonna say something, or the cat got your tongue," jeered Tobin. Robert appeared as white as a ghost, his body was shaking like a reed being blown left and right by strong winds. "Are you alright? you look like you have just seen a ghost," asked Rosie, she had calmed down by then. He paced up and down, then he replied," Iam alright, but I am not sure of what I have just seen. It's nothing, I didn't see anything, I thought I saw something, but there again I think it was my imagination running wild. "Never mind boy," declared John." Tell us about it when you are ready. The thing is, the bangings have stopped, and hopefully we can all go to bed assured just like before," declared John as the man of the house. He felt he had to exert some form of authority as it was his responsibility to look out for his family, he was in control. "I suggest we all go to bed, for Christ's sake we all could do with some good night's sleep. They all dispersed to bed respectively, and hoped for an undisturbed sleep, after all tomorrow was going to be another day. "Good night children, don't forget to put the fire out," he declared. He got Rosie, held her by the hand, and led her upstairs to bed. Rebecca, Tobin and Robert stayed up a bit longer stuck in the drawing room discussing the happenings they had just encountered. "You coward," expressed Tobin, "tell us what you saw in the garden," declared Tobin. "Uuum! I don't know where to start, I don't think you going to believe me," started Robert. "I looked round the front yard, and I didn't see anybody there, then I went to the back garden via the back gate, intially I didn't see anything extra ordinary until I got to the end of the garden, the torch didn't allow me much visibility," he panted. Rebecca immediately started talking about Ms Biggs what she had said to her and Rosie, Robert and Tobin were least surprised, because she had said it before a couple of times. The dots seemed to be fitting with what Charles had told them about the story of the cottage being haunted. "Charles seems to be a moron," expressed Tobin. Tobin being an avoidant of problems, he was least interested in the subject, he would rather nothing was happening within cottage. As the conversation carried on, he was becoming more and more flusterred, and he decided to go to bed, leaving Rebecca and Robert to carry on debating. He went to bed flustered, he didn't even bid them good night. He stomped upstairs and went straight to sleep, avoidance was his game, and it made him feel secure.

The following morning after John and the boys had left for work and college, Aida arrived at Bramwell, she brought a cake and cookies that she had baked that morning. She knocked at the door excitely. Rosie answered the door and led her to the kitchen were they chatted away until about lunch time. Ms Biggs turned up as well, she had sneaked in through the back gate and she was feeding the chickens. "What are you doing here Ms Biggs," asked Rosie; Aida became curious, she followed Rosie outside. "She had been coming here to feed the chickens before we moved here," said Rebecca to Aida, "So don't worry, we know her," she said. Rosie was talking to Ms Biggs. "It has become a matter of a habit, I am sorry if I have intruded," said Ms Biggs. "Don't be silly," replied Rosie, "after you have finished feeding them damn birds come in the kitchen and join us for a cup of coffee," Rosie replied gaily. She smiled and then turned away from Ms Biggs with a synical, annoyed crooked smile. "Alright then," replied Ms Biggs, "I notice you have got company," added Ms Biggs as she carried on feeding the chickens and Rosie walked away. She mumbled something to herself while she attended to the chickens. "Lord help us and save us," she said to herself. Aida was curious about the Lawrence family and what led them to move into Bramwell. "Your family intrigues me," she said to Rosie. "What made you move here? We moved here because of Justin's parents passing, and so we had to occupy their cottage, "Aida said without being asked. Rosie gave her a warm smile then replied, "It is because of my husband's job, he was made redundant and he found a job here. We used to live about fifty miles from here, and the opportunity came for him to be employed here," she replied. Then Ms Biggs walked into the kitchen were they were chatting and having coffee. "I hope I'm not intruding," she said gaily. Rosie introduced her to Aida, and told her that they were neighbours. "Pleased to meet you," she said as she shook hands with Aida. "So you are the family that moved in next door to Bramwell. Bramwell means a lot to this community. Are you Carlos' family?" she asked as if surprised. "We have heard stories about these two cottages," she looked downwards as if it were a condemnation to her of speaking about it. "Still, I am an old lady, I don't know what I am talking about but causing trouble. Never mind what I am talking about, it is all rubbish," she smiled. Rosie and Aida looked at each other speechless. Ms Biggs sipped on her coffee, and kept her head down, she felt uncomfortable. She sipped her last drop and then decided to leave. "I must dash, the church committee awaits, I do my voluntary there you see. If you don't mind Rebecca can see me out. What a lovely daughter you have got there Mrs L," smiled Ms Biggs. "Sure of cause," Rosie replied. "I hope to see you soon, and we can talk some more," added Rosie. Rebecca walked her out, instead of just seeing her to the door Rebecca decided to walk her half way to the local church. "Your house is haunted you know," started Ms Bigg's talking to Rebecca. "I have seen so many families perish in that house, and you are going to be the next," she said in an anxious voice. "I have seen them come and perish, because of the evil entity that dwells in there," she perpetuated. As they walked down the dust road that leads to the church, Rebecca was kicking the pebbles on the road, lost in contemplation. "The funny thing is that Ms Biggs, I believe every word you are saying, I have seen things and I have heard things in that house, I don't care what everybody else thinks, you are right," Rebecca replied. "I know," replied Ms Biggs, that is why I chose you to walk me out of the cottage because I had to tell you. I knew you would believe in me," she smiled. She reached out to Rebecca's hand, and held it tightly then said, "I believe in you, you can set your family free from that demon that dwells in your home. "Thank you Ms Biggs, I can always reach out to you if things get worse," she added. "You can count on that," she replied in a warm tone. She released her hand, "Iam almost there now, I don't want the two of us been seen together. Hurry now back home or else your mother might think I have kidnapped you," Ms Biggs said. "Now you know where you can reach me, I told you my address. Hurry back now," she said as she walked away. Rebecca stood there for a while motionless, shook her head and headed back to Bramwell. When she got home, Aida was also leaving, she said her goodbyes, but she was going to meet up with Rosie and the family at the barbecue which she was hosting that Saturday.

The Menderez's were busy preparing for the barbercue, Justin and the boys were to run the barbecue. They invited about twenty people from the village, and Roger and his family were going to be there as well, as well as the mayor and his family. Rosie got herself ready early, as she was interested in Ms Biggs, she decided to go pick her up and take her to the barbecue since it was a communal get together. She thought Ms Biggs being a widow with no family of her own, she thought that it would be a kind gesture taking her along. "I will see you at the Menderez's she said to her family as she went to pick Ms Biggs. It was quite a walk, the road was a bit rough, full of pebbles, and on top of that it was steep. She walked along expectantly, she went past the creek, and into Baldon road till she reached the opposite of Almer primary school, as Ms Biggs had said, and got to the house with a red front door, that was her house. She knocked and knocked but there was no response. She wasn't going to give up that easy, she walked round the back garden to the kitchen door, she peered through the kitchen window, and there was Ms Biggs sat at the table drinking coffee and eating a muffin. Rosie knocked on the window, Ms Biggs saw her and waved, then she went to open the door. "What a surprise!" she said, "what brings you here. Is something bad happening at your cottage! why are you here," she asked as she ushered Rosie into her kitchen. "I knocked and knocked at your front door! couldn't you hear the knock," said Rosie. She strolled back to her seat, "Not many people drop by, since my husband passed away. In fact you are the first visitor to knock on my door since his passing. What is it you want?" she asked. Rosie sat herself comfortably on one of the old chairs in the kitchen. "Coffee or tea?" Ms Biggs asked grinning away. "No thank you Ms Biggs, I am here to take you to a barbecue the Menderez's are hosting today. There is going to be many people there from this community, I thought you might want to come," Rosie expressed. "I hope you don't mind," she cooed. Ms Biggs smiled again, as she pulled another one of the old chairs to park her fat bottom. She had a habit of not sitting in the same chair for long. "I never get invited to any functions here, I don't know why. I think they don't trust me, I am not one of their cult members," stated Ms Biggs. "You see I am not one of them," cried Ms Biggs. "What do you mean cult?" questioned Rosie. Rosie looked around Ms Biggs kitchen, it appeared very eccentric, full of old furniture with a couple of pictures on the wall. They were pictures of her husband who had passed away a good ten years prior. "Who is that on the pictures?" asked Rosie, "Are they pictures of your late husband," she enquired. "Yes that is my poor Cecil he died of lung cancer, and left me a widow. I have no children of my own, I have spent most of my days volunteering at some kids home, and our local church. I have been volunteering for a good years now," she said solemnly. "I am sorry Ms Biggs," said Rosie. "Well, don't worry about it," it was many years ago that he passed," she replied. "Are you coming then to the barbecue," asked Rosie. Ms Biggs got up to straighten her bones, she couldn't sit down for a long time on a hard chair. "I guess then, but I am going there for you. None of them like me here, that's why I wasn't invited; that's just that to it," replied Ms Biggs. She took her empty cup and plate and reached for the sink to wash up, "I want to tell you a story," she said. "Please tell me a story," replied Rosie. "Mmmm, very well," said Ms Biggs. "Many years ago when I was a little girl growing up in this village, Bramwell cottage was derilique. Years passed then soon it started having occupants," she heaved. "Each family that moved in there perished, one by one, that is when the rumours started going round that it was haunted. Nobody from that cottage ever got out alive. Each and every one of them perished, some say it is a satanic cult in operation that killed them. They believe the cult was started by a father Santos many years ago, and that it has carried through to present day," she proceeded. "So far there has been six generations that have perished in that cottage, and many more before my time," she continued. "The family before you all perished, except one, a young woman by the name of Suzanna. The entity consumed your former neighbours as well, a sweet old couple, relations of your present neighbours," Ms Biggs said. "Now I have said it, I will get my self ready and we shall go to the barbecue. Remember I am doing it for you," she hissed and then disappeared to the bathroom to get herself ready for the event.

By the time Rosie and Ms Biggs got to the Menderez's the barbecue was in full swing. They were the last to show up. Rosie's family were already there alongside the others.

Chapter 3

Justin was a man of formidable character, bold in nature and a bit forward, forceful guy, who expected everyone to respect him. He was a bit devious, calculating and impetuous, despite being highly sociable. He was in his fifties, and was rather aging too quickly, his hair was grey, and he was heavily bolding. His eyes were dark and narrowed like a serpent's, and yet he was very sociable, possibly to mask his devious character. He was quite tall and large in stature. His top half layed a big burden to his thin legs, and his skin looked more like rubber, he was pale and mysterious. He had small hands and big feet, his top half was a lot larger than the bottom, so often he would drag his feet when walking. His wife Aida was more loving, consciencious of others, respectful and patient in nature. She was a short plump woman, who weighed about sixteen and half stone, and no more than five feet tall. She had big green eyes and a small sharp nose, her hair was blonde just like Trevor's. She had a big flat bottom that always showed when she wore trousers, of which she often did.

When Rosie and Ms Biggs arrived, the barbecue was in full swing, they were greeted by Roger and his wife, "It's nice to have you here," said Roger. "Rosie!" he said, "already swimming with the sharks," he smirked as he walked away to talk to John. Rosie appeared nervous, "Do you know all these people," she asked Ms Biggs. Ms Biggs gave a crooked smile, "I know them like a fitting glove," she responded. "Stick with me, and soon you will learn," she said. "Oh! oh! there is Rebecca! get her here!" sparked Ms Biggs, "because I want the pair of you to observe," she gleed. She had spotted Rebecca chatting to Trevor and Charles the Menderez's boys. Rosie got distructed when Roger came up to her to have a chat. "Can I steal Rosie from you for a minute," said Roger to Ms Biggs, "I want to introduce her to the

Mayor. "Of cause," replied Ms Biggs. Rosie went off with Roger while Ms Biggs went to talk to Rebecca. Rebecca was too distracted by the Menderez's boys, so she didn't talk long with Ms Biggs, she quickly excused herself. "This is our Mayor," said Roger as he introduced Rosie to Mayor Jenkins, he was with his wife and three children, two boys and a girl. Mayor Jenkins' wife was a timid woman named Sheila, she appeared to be in her mid fifties. She was grey haired, a bit on the plump side, and humble; she was very eager to meet Rosie. "How do you like it here, and have you settled in yet," she said with a beautiful cheerful smile on her face. You are going to being seeing a lot of my husband around because he is a very active member of our community here. Rosie shook her hand, and what a strong hand shake it was. After the introductions Mayor Jenkins disappeared in the crowd to find John, and left Rosie with his wife Sheila. They talked and talked mainly about their families. Like Rosie her two boys were in their early twenties and still living at home. "We have got something in common, two grown boys, and so does Aida. I hope that our boys become friends, they all seem to be good boys," exclaimed Rosie. "You are right," responded Sheila, she was sipping on her wine while munching on cocktail sausages, and some other finger foods. They were lost in conversation, while Rebecca indulged herself in the company of the boys. Somehow they had grouped together, her, the Menderez's boys, her brothers and the Mayor's boys. All they spoke about was Bramwell and the strange phenomenas happening there. Charles was a lot like his father Justin, very serious, calculating and a bit devious in nature, though he was very differrent in physical appearance. In appearance he was more like his mother, short in stature and some how plump. He had green eyes like his mother except his eyes were larger and more closer to each other, and had blonde hair. He loved his father more than he loved his mother and brother. He was very loyal to him, and whatever Justin said and did, it was always right in the eyes Charles. Whereas to Trevor, he was the complete opposite, Trevor was a mummy's boy. He loved his mother more than anybody in his life, even his previous girlfriends had to come second. Trevor was tall like his father, he was a fun loving young man, always sincere and and somewhat too trusting, that came from his mother. "So you think your cottage is haunted then," asked one of the Jenkins' boys. "Yes I have seen and heard strange things," replied Rebecca, "we all have in the family, isn't that right Tobin," said Rebecca. "Besides the banging noises, I saw something in the bottom of the garden," exclaimed Robert. "It was a group of people dressed in black robes, and the leader wore a red robe. I didn't get close enough to see who they were, but they all disappeared into thin air as if they were never. I was confused," continued Robert anxiously. His heart started beating fast and his palms sweating, he was panting for breathe. "It is nothing, don't dwell on it," reassured Charles. "Thanks," replied Robert with a smile. "Nit wit here thinks I am a coward," he said playfully kicking his brother in the ass. John was going to divulge anything and everything to anybody at the barbecue about their experiences at Bramwell. He heard a lot of things, but he chose to keep his cards close to his chest. Somewhere deep inside Rosie lay suspicion about the people there at the barbecue, she saw Roger pull Justin away, she followed them discreetly in the house. They went into the drawing room and shut the door, she tried eeves dropping but she couldn't hear anything as the door was tightly shut, they were whispering. She left the house and went looking for Ms Biggs. Ms Biggs was looking like a fish out of water, nobody was talking to her, infact she was contemplating on leaving the barbecue, till Rosie came to her. "Something is going on," Rosie said to Ms Biggs. "I saw Roger drag Justin into the house. "I followed them, and they went into some room, and they shut the door, I wasn't able to hear anything but I am suspicious," she panted. "I told you, didn't I." Ms Biggs thrust her index finger on Rosie's forehead, "watch and observe, I keep telling you," Ms Biggs said in a patronising tone. "They are after your family," she warned, "don't trust any of them," she insisted. Ms Biggs had been wondering solo at the barbecue, her only friend was Rosie, none of them wanted to talk to her, they saw her as nothing other than trouble for the community. When Roger came out of the drawing room with Justin, his attention was back on Rosie, he stole Rosie once again from Ms Biggs. Rosie was resciprocative, she did that in the name of trying to get information from Roger. "Stay away from that woman," he said, warning Rosie from Ms Biggs. "She is nothing but trouble in the community, she will lend you in hot soup if you are not careful. She destroyed the former occupants of your home. She caused so much trouble for them that up today nobody knows what happened to them," he said in a stern voice. Rosie grew nervous, "I believe you," she said, "she is totally mental," she nodded. "I hear she has been feeding your chickens, don't allow her in your property, you need to lock the back gate," said Roger in a scary tone. "I understand," responded Rosie. "I am going to find your husband and tell him the same, to stay away from her, and that if she causes trouble, I will have to deal with her," declared Roger. He left to find John in the crowd, he found John talking to Mayor Jenkins. Mayor Jenkins was busy talking about the charities he supports through fundraising, and the work he does trying to keep the community together. "I like you John, and I want you to be part of our close community," he said, "but I urge you to stay away from that Ms Biggs." John was a bit perplexed, "I hear you Mayor," he replied hesitantly, he was rubbing his hair in a nervous way. "I am glad Mayor, I will bare that in mind," he shook hands with the Mayor. Time was moving on, it was beginning to darken, so John regathered his family and decided to leave even though the party was still in full swing. The truth of the matter is that, John grew more suspicious of them, all that he was quite happy to take his family away from there. In his mind, he did not want any of them to be involved with that community. Roger and the Mayor went looking for Justin, they got him in the house, and they headed for the basement whispering amongst each other. It was the big black book that got them together, they had to hide it somewhere, and Justin's basement seemed to be the right place. How quickly Justin had aquainted himself with the locals. He was either being manipulated or he was part of it. They went into the basement, and somewhere on the basement floor lay an opening with a little door, it had been designed to hide things. They pulled the carpet, opened the little door and they placed the book in there, and then covered it back up, they pulled the carpet back as if nothing was hidden beneath. Everything was done quite discreetly, nobody noticed, and that is what made Roger and the Mayor happy.

John took his family back to Bramwell, it was going to be a long night, by then it was about 11pm. They spoke about the barbecue and everything bizzaire they came across. "I think Ms Biggs is a nice lady, she is trying to warn us about something," cried Rosie. "I agree with mum," instated Rebecca, "I like her, and I think she is a genuinely caring person," she proceeded. John was pacing up and down the drawing room in front of the open fire. "It's her mumbo jumbo rubbish that is causing us to be in this state, from now on, she is banned from this house; do you hear that Rosie!" he stated. Rosie simply walked away from John, and went to the kitchen to fix herself a cup of coffee. Tobin, Rebecca, and Robert decided to call it a night, and left John in the drawing room contemplating. Rosie sat in the kitchen drinking her coffee, then afterwards she went to bed. John sat in the drawing room for a good couple of hours thinking. He thought of selling Bramwell, and moving back to the city, it was hard core. Eventually John retired to bed.

It was a ritual for the Lawrence family to sit together at the dinner table for breakfast every Sunday morning, never mind lunch time each one will be doing their own thing, eating at whatever time suited them. They were sat at the table, except for Rebecca, Rosie shouted from the kitchen as she normally do, "Breakfast is ready," she shouted. She shouted and shouted for Rebecca to come downstairs, but there was no response. "She must be extremely tired," said Rosie to John as they started on their breakfast without her. They finished eating, but there was still no sign of Rebecca. It got to lunch time, but she still hadn't surfaced from upstairs. "I better go up there and see if she is alright," said Rosie to the boys who were messing about on the piano in the drawing room. Rosie went upstairs and knocked on Rebecca's door, there was no answer, she knocked some more, and still there was no answer. She opened the door, to her horror Rebecca was huddled in a corner and curled up like a ball, she looked scared. "Whatever is the matter with you?" cried Rosie. She went up to Rebecca and cuddled her. "What's going on?" she asked. Rebecca pointed at the fire place, she was speechless and shaking. "Talk to me, what is the matter? what is at the fireplace?" asked Rosie. She shook Rebecca over and over again, "Talk to me," she said again. Rebecca got up, she was still pointing at the fire place, breathing heavily. She said, "It's an old woman, she spoke to me." "What woman! there is nobody there!" cried Rosie. "She was there! I saw her!" replied Rebecca. "There is nobody there sweetheart, I will call your father to search your room if you like," said Rosie. "John! John! come up here now!" shouted Rosie. John was busy in the drawing room, reading the Sunday paper. He frowned then shouted back from downstairs, "What is it this time! is it Ms Biggs again! I have got no time for that nonsense." "Just come up! it's Rebecca!" shouted Rosie. He folded the paper neatly and laid on the side table, then he went upstairs. "What is going on," ha asked calmly. He saw Rebecca appearing highly anxious. "Ask your daughter, lest you call me dillusional, ask her," responded Rosie. John looked in the room, there was nothing puzzling at all. "What's going on Rebecca?" he asked. "There was some old woman in my room, she spoke to me," replied Rebecca. "I think it's a ghost. Dad this house is haunted just like Ms Biggs and the Menderez's boys said," she continued. Rebecca was calm by then. "She spoke to me," she added. "That is nonsense! there is no old woman here," replied John, he sounded cross. "You are listening a lot to that Ms Biggs! I don't want her here again! do you understand, the pair of you! next time she comes here just ring the police! understood!" he exclaimed before going back downstairs to read the paper. "Come have something to eat dear, you missed breakfast, you could do with some lunch, then we can talk more about it," comforted Rosie. "Come downstairs dear," said Rosie as she ushered Rebecca to the kitchen, Rosie was nervous. She was thinking of finding an exorcist or a priest to help them deal with whatever was going on in their house. She made some scrambled eggs on toast for Rebecca, sat her at the table while she had coffee. She sat with her, and observed her behaviour. Rebecca was distant in thought, all she did was stare at her breakfast. "I am not eating those eggs, they are poisoned and tainted with evil," she said. She looked at Rosie, more like staring at her without moving her eyes. She stared at her mother for ages without speaking a word. "They are telling me that Ms Biggs is evil, and that she has been feeding those chickens poison," she said to Rosie without blinking her eyes. Her eyes were fixated on Rosie's face, which made

Rosie extremely nervous. "Who is they?" asked Rosie. "It's the men in the robes, they gather in the bottom of the garden every night," replied Rebecca. "They are calling for me, and all of us, they are saying come join us at the bottom of the garden," slurred Rebecca. "Do you know them now?" asked Rosie. "They have been talking to me continually since I woke up, and I can hear them now. Shhhh, they are talking now, I must listen to them," she whispered. Rosie was perplexed, and tried persuading Rebecca to eat. "I am not hungry!" she yelled, "I must listen attentively, they say it is important that I listen to them," she started pacing up and down and whispering, "Ms Biggs is evil," she kept repeating. She started pulling her hair, and kept repeating, "Ms Biggs is evil! we must go to the bottom of the garden because they are waiting." Rosie called John, he came in to the kitchen reluctantly. "What is it this time," he said. "I think your daughter needs help, I am afraid she is losing it," said Rosie. "What are you talking about, she looks fine to me, she only needs to eat something and she will be fine," responded John reluctantly. "She is hearing voices, you hang around and see for yourself," said Rosie. John waited, then he saw it for himself, Rebecca started pacing up and down talking about the men in the robes. "We need a doctor, call a doctor," he said to Rosie. "Rebecca sweetheart do you want to talk about," persuaded John. Rebecca wasn't even hearing him, she kept pacing up and down. "We must go right away," she kept repeating herself. "Go where?" questioned Rosie. "We must go, they are talking to me," she said repeatedly. Rosie went to the phone to ring Dr Peters who was the local Doctor, while John tried to help Rebecca. Tobin and Robert heard what was going on in the kitchen that they left their rooms and came downstairs to the kitchen to find out. While Rosie was on the phone the boys tried talking to Rebecca, but she was way gone, now hallucinating. She was seeing men dressed in black robes, she ran out of the kitchen to her bedroom, there she huddled in a corner. Robert followed her, there she was seeing the old woman again, the old woman was talking to her, "Help us, help us," the old woman said. Robert couldn't see her. "There is nobody there, why don't you try and get into bed and get some rest," said Robert softly. He helped her into bed, and then he sat on her bed waiting for the Doctor to arrive. Dr Peters turned up, and Rosie led him to Rebecca's room. He examined her. He couldn't find anything physically wrong with her, but it was all in her mind. He told Rosie and John to take her to the local hospital. "The hallucinations could be temporary, and there again not, it is hard to tell, at least in hospital she will get the adequete help. There are good Doctors there" said Dr Peters before he left. Rosie and John did as they were advised, they got Rebecca ready and they took her to the local hospital. The waiting was long but eventually they were called in to the consultation room. They were called in by a young Doctor called Edelbert, he was quite charismatic, and in his late twenties. He examined Rebecca in the presence of Rosie and John, his conclusion was again, that nothing was wrong with her physically but that the problem lay in her mind. "Has she suffered anything traumatic of late?" he asked John and Rosie. John and Rosie looked at each other, "No Doctor, but she has been seeing things that are not there, and hearing voices," Rosie responded while holding John's hand. John squeezed Rosie's hand, he appeared hopeful that the Doctor might tell them what was wrong with their daughter. When Dr Edelbert looked at the nurse's notes who had filled in Rebecca's details, he got a shock of his life to see that her address was Bramwell cottage. His mouth went ajar, he started fiddling with the paper work uncontrollably in a nervous manner. "You live at Bramwell cottage!" he said, "I thought that cottage was empty, forgive me I had no idea that there was new occupants," he continued. "Yeh! we are the new occupants, infact we moved in a few weeks!" blutted John. "Anyways, I am giving her a prescription of anti anxiety medication, that should do the trick alongside a bit of TLC," said the Doctor. After Rosie took the prescription, she thanked Doctor Edelbert, and they walked out, John was holding Rebecca's hand. Dr Edelbert took a sigh, then he shook his head, "Not again! it can't be happening again," he whispered to himself, then he went on to call for his next patient. He had a lot to think about, he thought mainly about Suzanna. Rosie, Rebecca and John got home, they were exhausted and Rebecca took her first dose of medication and went to bed. After work Doctor Edelbert gathered his thoughts then guts and decided to call Suzanna. She was busy chatting to auntie Doris when the phone rang. She was shocked to hear from him, she was busy trying to bury the experience of Bramwell and move on. "Why are you calling me?" she asked Doctor Edelbert. "Suzanna! listen carefully, I think it's happening again," he paused, "your new occupants at Bramwell, they are experiencing what your family experienced," he paused again. "Today I saw a young woman experiencing phenomenas who is dwelling in that cottage. I fear it is happening again," he paused for a response. Auntie Doris was sitting with Rebecca in the lounge where one of the house phones was. She took a sigh, "Hold on, I think I should take this call in my bedroom," she said. She placed the phone on the side and she dashed upstairs to pick up the call from there. "Auntie Doris, this is a private call, can you put the phone down when I pick it up from upstairs," she requested. "Okay dear," she replied. She held the phone, and when Suzanna picked up the phone in her room auntie Doris did not put the phone down in the lounge, she decided to eeves drop because she wanted to know what was going on. "What shall we do, because me I don't want to be involved, I have been through enough hell. What do you want to do?" Suzanna gasped. Doctor Edelbert took a big breathe, "I don't know Suzanna, this is way beyond me, but we can't leave them like that," he sighed. "Why don't you meet up with me next weekend, I will be free then, or I will pick you up, what do you think," he expressed. "Mmmm I don't know, let us meet up for coffee first, then we will decide from there. Suzanna agreed to be picked up from her auntie's house that following Saturday. In the mean time back at Bramwell things seemed to be settled Rebecca was still asleep, Rosie was portering around, and John and the boys were doing some gardening. Ms Biggs didn't turn up to feed the chickens, attending the barbecue at the Menderez's left her scared to be anywhere near Bramwell. Robert fed the chickens, there was about three dozen chickens in the coop, and they supplied the family with at least a dozen eggs each day. Since the Lawrence's had been at Bramwell less than a while, they hardly knew that there was chickens at the bottom of the garden, it had been Ms Biggs feeding them all along, once they knew and the large supply of eggs, Rosie thought of selling some of the eggs at the local market. Their back garden stretched for ages that it was no less than two and half acres. The chickens had previous owners, the Thomson family. The knowledge that the Lawrence family had about the Thomsons was that they had left abruptly because of a family tragedy. Rosie had been trying hard to keep herself busy that afternoon by portering, she received a letter from Ms Biggs. Ms Biggs had written that letter and posted it threw their letter box. She had written the letter on the day she met Rosie and Rebecca for the first time when she was feeding the chickens, but had kept it in her drawers. The letter read,,,,' Dear Rosie, I am praying for your family. The house you are living in is cursed,,, they want your souls. I urge you to take your family out and leave,,,,,ps Ms Biggs. The letter came in a very old envelope with tea stains on it. Ms Biggs was a frugile woman who never threw away anything, obviously that envelope had been sitting in one of her drawers for many years judging by the state of it. By and by throughout her life she had grown to be self reliant, and self sufficient. Rosie was perplexed by the letter, she showed it to John, and they vowed not to speak of it to anybody.

 The days that followed there was peace at Bramwell, Rebecca had gotten better, and the whole family was flourishing. The boys were enjoying college, Tobin's plan was to finish college and become a motor mechanic, wheras Robert wanted to become an electrician. They made friends and even girl friends. Tobin started seeing Mayor Jenkins daughter Rachel, while Robert was still looking. Robert be-friended a few girls but wasn't exactly settled with one. Mayor Jenkins was even welcoming Tobin at his house. He met Rachel in college, she was studying to be a beautician, he met her via one of his friends who had introduced her to him. Before long they became inseparable, often Rachel would come for dinner at the Lawrences. Rosie and Rebecca liked her very much that she became like part of the family. In between them days Doctor Edelbert went to pick Suzanna up from auntie Doris'. Auntie Doris fell in love with Doctor Edelbert's charm from the moment he introduced himself, she couldn't stop flattering him. Suzanna hadn't explained to her that he had been Sophia's boyfriend, she marely introduced him as an old friend. She felt it wasn't necessary for her to know all the details. Besides her eeves dropping she did not hear anything out of the extraordinary, they had kept their conversation to a minimal when they spoke on the phone. She kept offering food, from the humble pear to the most expensive wine she had in the house, of which he declined politely. He kept insisting that he wasn't stopping by for long, he had only come to pick Suzanna up and be off. They left auntie Doris in an excitable mood, it had been good for her to have somebody stop by her house as she hardly ever had guests come round. Doctor Edelbert took Suzanna to his house where they could talk peacefully without any noise nor interruptions. They were both worried about the Lawrences, Suzanna decided to stay with Doctor Edelbert until they figured out a way to help the Lawrence family. "I wonder what happened to Father Dowling?" asked Doctor Edelbert. "I don't know, I hope they didn't go after him and killed him," replied Suzanna. "He is a smart man, I am sure he left the village, and possibly at some monestary somewhere, with his fellow priests, talking about us. Suzanna and Edelbert decided to do some more research about Bramwell, before they could take any action to help the Lawrence family.

Back at Bramwell, John was out at work and the boys in college, Rebecca hadn't shown up for breakfast and Rosie was appearing concerned. Rosie went upstairs to check on her, her bedroom was locked from the inside. "Rebecca! Rebecca! open up!" she shouted repeatedly, but there was no answer. It was surprising to her because none of the bedrooms in the cottage came with keys, so obviously it was impossible to lock any one of those bedroom doors, what could it have been. "Rebecca!!!!" she shouted over and over again, but still there was no reply. She ran to John's garage which was on the side of the cottage, thankfully the garage door was open, she looked around to see if she could find any tools to open Rebecca's bedroom door. She found a massive sledge hammer, and an axe. She grabbed the two, and raced back upstairs to Rebecca's bedroom door to try and bash it in. First she used the sledge hammer knocking the door, but the door did not open. Then she moved on to the axe, she wacked the side of the door several times till the door opened. When she entered a swam of flies flew out, nearly blinding her that she ran downstairs and outside through the front door, the flies followed her outside then vanished into thin air. She was scared for a while but she was determined to save Rebecca, she gathered her stamina then went back into the house, went back upstairs. She got into Rebecca's room, she saw her naked, lying on top of the bed appearing lifeless. Her body was covered in bruises and weird markings. The bedroom white wall paper were covered in blood writings, weird symbols and signs, and there was scratchings on the wall paper. "Jesus Christ!" said Rosie, she covered Rebecca up with a blanket. She shook her, shouting Rebecca!Rebecca! wake up! she continued, eventually Rebecca woke up. "Are you alright! She sat upright she looked dazed and confused. "Here put some clothes on," she said as she handed her some clothes. Rebecca kept staring at the writings on the wall, that Rosie had to help her dress. Immediately Rosie heard whistling coming from downstairs, she helped Rebecca up, then got her out of the room. They went downstairs to the lounge, and the whistling continued. Rebecca was sat down and all she did was staring around specifically on the wall paper, she didn't say a word. Rosie followed the whistling to see where it was coming from, It was coming from the drawing room, and she could smell tobacco. She went back to attending to Rebecca. She rung John, and asked him to come home at once. His workplace was only a couple of miles away. The taps in the kitchen started running by themselves, and she heard rustling of saucepans, and yet there was nobody in the kitchen. The whistling moved from the drawing room to the kichen and the whiff of tobacco followed, Rosie then heard footsteps going up the stairs. She didn't dare follow the footsteps lest it was something dangerous, instead she chose to stay with Rebecca till John came home. John drove home immediately, he noticed that he was being followed by a beige jeep, he couldn't quite see who was behind the wheel, presumably it was a man. He followed him from work and all the way home. When he turned into Bramwell drive, the truck sped past. "Come on in fast! it's Rebecca!" she gasped, she grabbed him by the hand and led him into the lounge where Rebecca had been sitting for the past hour. "She seems to be all sorts," John said, he was highly concerned but faked composure. "Did you call the Doctor, because that Doctor Edelbert said we should ring him if her condition worsens. "I wanted you to be here to see for yourself before I called the Doctor. Go up to her room and see, and tell me what you make of it," exclaimed Rosie. Before he went to her room, he tried communicating with Rebecca, but she did not respond, she remained in a vacant state. He then dashed up to her room, upon entering he was dismayed, he shook his head then went back downstairs. "What is that?" he asked Rosie, "who did that?" he asked some more. Rosie explained to him what had happened, she even spoke of the flies knowing that John wouldn't believe her. Many a time he had made her second guess herself because of his compulsive nature. John was thinking that it was Rebecca who painted the weird writings on the wall, however he couldn't explain the scratchings on the wall because they were definitely nail scratchings. If she had scratched the walls her fingers would be bleeding. "Call Doctor Edelbert straight away, and explain to him what has been going on," he said to Rosie. Rebecca was getting feverish, and started hallucinating again, Rosie rang the hospital and spoke to Doctor Edelbert who send an ambulance. Since the hospital was less busy, Doctor Edelbert decided to join the ambulance crew, partly because he was curious to see what was going on at Bramwell, and partly because he feared for Rebecca's life. The ambulance arrived and Doctor Edelbert dashed into the house while the ambulance crew followed behind. Somehow he felt that inorder to help Rebecca he had to re-visit Bramwell so that he can make proper evaluation. Before he even saw Rebecca, Rosie led him to her room. What he saw reminded him of his experiences with the Thomson family, seeing the writings on the wall and weird symbols, scratchings on the wall and the hallucinations Rebecca was experiencing. The ambulance crew was attending to Rebecca, checking her vital signs and so on, Doctor Edelbert pulled Rosie and John aside. They went to the kitchen, and he started talking about the Thomson family. "I believe this is supernatural," he urged, "you need an exorcist, because this is beyond my healing arts," he insisted. John didn't buy the story, he requested that Rebecca should be taken into a hospital where she would get appropriate help. "Very well," said Doctor Edelbert, "if you ever change your mind, here is my private number. You can reach me at home on this number, or you can catch me at the hospital," he said. He left John and Rosie and asked the paramedics to take Rebecca to the hospital for admission. Rebecca was admitted on a general ward where Doctor Edelbert regurlary worked, he worked on a rotational system as the hospital was very small, catering for a small population. Suzanna was still staying with Doctor Edelbert. While he was at work she would keep herself occupied by visiting the local library. John was a stubborn man, he needed more proof to be convinced, so Rosie decided to pay a visit to Ms Biggs, she went alone, by then Rebecca had been in hospital for a few days. She didn't say anything to John, so she walked to Ms Biggs, she walked up the hill got to the creek, and opposite Almer primary school then she was there, Baldon road. From the outside there didn't seem to be much life appearing from her cottage, all the curtains were closed, and there was total silence. She knocked on that red door multiple times, till eventually Ms Biggs appeared. She appeared worn out. "Come on in," she said politely, "I knew you would come, I have been expecting you," she said in a warm tone of voice. Rosie went in. "Do you want a cup of tea or coffee?" she asked politely. "Coffee please, no sugar," replied Rosie as she sat on one of the hard chairs in the kitchen. "How do you manage?" questioned Rosie. "Manage what?" responded Ms Biggs. "To live in this village," said Rosie, "how do you do it," she carried on. "I believe everything that you told me about this village, but how do you do it, I mean staying here and yet you know all this," she added. "It's old age I guess, I am an old woman, and I have got nothing to lose, that is why," smiled Ms Biggs as she sat herself down on the hard chair. Rosie sipped on her coffee in wonderment. "Do you care for a muffin, I baked them early this morning. They are really good, you can't miss on that," she smiled further as she moved the muffin plate over towards Rosie. "Try them they are really good, it's an old family recipe. My mother passed it on to me, and she inherited it from her grandmother." Have one, it won't hurt you," she insisted. "Very well then Ms Biggs," replied Rosie as she reached out for a muffin. She munched on the muffin while contemplating and listening to Ms Biggs at the same time. "I believe you, but John will never accept it, he thinks it's a bunch of mumbo jambo nonsense. What can I do to convince him?" she wallowed. "You can't do anything to convince him, let him find out for himself. As time goes on, he will begin to see that what you have been telling him is true. Don't push him, don't even think about it, time will reveal all," said Ms Biggs smiling away. "You think so, I hope you are right," replied Rosie. Ms Biggs got up from the old chair, stretched her bones for a while, then sat back down. "You see I have to keep getting up and stretching, otherwise my bones stiffen up," she smiled. "One day you will be old like me, and you will know what I am talking about," she smirked. "My husband was a strong man, he could not give up easily, he fought that cancer right to the end of his life. Listen, You have got to fight for your family just like my old Cecil did with his cancer," she proceeded. "But how can I do that, I am not familiar to this sort of thing, you are," replied Rosie in a soft manner. Ms Biggs jiggled again, her back was killing her, "Let's move into the lounge, the sofas are comfortable for me there because I want to tell you something," she said. They moved to the lounge where Ms Biggs had her own settee which was good for her back. "Ever since I met you, I have been fearing for my life. Here in this village lies a cult, and more or less everybody here is associated with the cult, or at least supports it. If they smell you are going to be a problem to them, they eliminate you. I have been followed about, and I feel they get in my home when I am not around. I have been experiencing extensive noises around my property. They have been flashing their car headlamps right inside my house, and hooting their horns everytime they pass by. It has been herondeous, they murdered my cat. One day I came home and found poor Ms jinx dead right on my porch. Ms Jinx was the name of my cat whom I had for ages; to come home and find him dead on the porch was devastating. He had knife stabbings all over his body. I believe it was a message from them for me to stay away from you and Bramwell. They are dangerous; since I am an old lady, I have got nothing to lose, but I warn you to be extremely careful, and vigilant," she paused. "My old Cecil would have none of it, that is why I think they poisoned him to death, he didn't die of cancer. He stood up against them and their practices, so they killed him. "They trust everybody else around here except me, because of Cecil. They have been watching me, stalking me everywhere I go, so be careful, they want to sacrifice your family, it is their tradition to sacrifice any family that moves into Bramwell. Why is that, it is because Bramwell was home to Father Santos, the founder of the satanic cult. He died over one hundred years ago, but his religion carries on, every few years they appoint a new leader. The entity is inside your daughter, and you must save her. I would like to visit her in the hospital, but they are watching me," she paused, and took a few seconds break before she proceeded. "It is Roger now who is the leader of all this, be careful of him. And those neighbours of yours, his father was a big part of it; does the name Carlos ring a bell. He hid tonnes of the cults artefacts; his son lives there now, be careful of them as well. Don't trust anybody here, your family is marked for sacrifice by the whole village. If you can get out, do so now, or else it will all end in disaster," proceeded Ms Biggs. "Now I have said it all, go home now and look after your family," she smiled. "Don't worry about a poor old lady, there is nothing left in this world for me; you know where to find me if you need me," she said as she ushered Rosie out of her house. That was the last she ever heard from Ms Biggs before she was found dead, impaled at the Abbey ruins. It was a ritual sacrifice, when she was found, she was wearing her night gown, it meant that the ritual happened either at night, or early hours of the morning when there wasn't anybody to witness the crime. The local police couldn't make any sense of it, why would anybody have a tiff with an old lady, it didn't make sense. Some believed that the local police knew who did it, and that they were part of the cult. Bare in mind that not everybody in the village was part of the cult. There was families who kept themselves to themselves, and played no part in the village politics. Some locals believed that their local police were working for Mayor Jenkins, and could have been easily gagged. When Rosie heard about the news, she was devastated, she felt hopeless, the only person she trusted was now dead, and died a horrible death. Suzanna and Doctor Edelbert heard of the news, they attended her funeral. They felt it was time for them to reveal some hidden secret to the Lawrence family. Suzanna was going to tell them who she was, and explain to them what happened to her family. The police didn't get anywhere in trying to catch the criminals responsible for Ms Biggs' death, there just wasn't any leads. Soon after the funeral, Doctor Edelbert and Suzanna plucked up enough courage to knock on the Lawrences' cottage. It was about three in the afternoon that they both knocked on the door. Rosie came to answer the door, to her dismay it was Doctor Edelbert. "What can I do for you Doctor?" she asked in pleperxity, "and who is that?" she was reffering to Suzanna. "What brings you here?" she asked again. "May we come in," he said. "Ms Biggs was a good friend of yours, and so was she my patient, so don't be surprised with you seeing me at her funeral. This is my friend Suzanna, she used to live here. Iam sure we have got something important to tell you." Suzanna introduced her self. "Well! come on in, somehow I am not surprised to see her here. I think it is time for some explanation on what is going on in this village," she said. She led them to the drawing room. The drawing room, it was always a good reception area for guests, according to Rosie. It was cozy, calm and homely. The fire was ablaze, and every settee was comfortable unlike Ms Biggs old furniture. "I think you two should get aquiented." Suzanna and her family lived here before you moved in. Her family became victim of some occult happening here, and I fear Rebecca's condition is not merely a medical one but spiritual," Doctor Edelbert said to Rosie. She made them cups of tea while they chatted. Suzanna explained to Rosie every detail of what her family went through, right up to their demise. "I loved my family, and they all perished because of this cottage," said Suzanna, she started sobbing uncontrollably. She asked if she could tour around the cottage, for memories sake. John was at work, and the boys in college, so she was all alone. Rosie took them round the cottage, "What about the chickens, are they still here," she asked. "Yes they are, and we are taking good care of them," she replied. Them seeing Rebecca's bedroom covered in blood writing and all the weird symbols, Edelbert and Suzanna were the least shocked. "Mmmm, this is not surprising, I kind of expected all this," she muttered to herself. "You need to move out of this house, or else you will perish like my family did," said Suzanna. "Do you know what happened to Ms Biggs, obviously it has got something to do with cult. Do you know who did it, and why," enquired Rosie. "They never trusted her, even when my family was still here, they killed her for snitching," replied Suzanna confidently. "They saw her as a danger to the community. If anybody was going to tell the outside world about their cult, it would have been Ms Biggs, so they kept her on watch all the time," added Suzanna. "Is my Rebecca going to get better?" she asked, her face was looking bewildered and scared. "We are going to help you, but we can't guarantee anything. Doctor Edelbert helped my family so much, he is more than just a physician," said Suzanna. "To begin with, I was in wonderment myself till I saw with my own eyes that supernatural activities are real," he interjected. "I believe, it's happening again," he added. "Things got so bad that we had to involve some priests, mainly Father Francis, but unfortunately he perished as well after attempting an exorcism," exclaimed Doctor Edelbert. "Who found Ms Biggs impaled?" asked Suzanna. "It was an old villager walking his dog. It was early hours of the morning that he found her, that's what we heard," replied Rosie. "Soon after he found her, he rang the police straight away, and he went knocking on his neighbours doors informing them of what he had seen. The neighbours did the same, informed their neighbours till the whole village knew. They all gathered at the Abbey ruins, just staring at Ms Biggs till the police turned up and took her down from the torture stake. There hasn't been any leads to connotate who did it," continued Rosie. "A few days ago, I received a letter from Ms Biggs warning me that my family is in danger, and that we should leave the village at once. Then when I went to see her, she was scared for her life, she thought the cult members were going to kill her purely because she spoke to me," Rosie explained. "The police have got no leads, however some villager claimed to have seen some activity happening at the Abbey ruins the night before Ms Biggs was found there. He told the police that he saw men wearing hooded robes at the ruins and that they were holding fire torches, and dancing in circles. He said it was like a ceremony happening there," Rosie sighed. "What is going on here Doctor," she questioned Edelbert. "I can't tell you, because my knowledge is very minimal, but what I can tell you is that Suzanna and I experienced similar experiences, so you are not alone," he said in a gentle voice. He put his arm around Rosie and said, "Do not be afraid, you are not alone." "We got help from a priest, and that is what we going to do. We are here to help you so that the troubles stop. We are going to find a priest and get rid of this problem once and for all," insisted Suzanna. "That is right," reassured Doctor Edelbert. Edelbert and Suzanna left Rosie feeling hopeful, despite the fact that Rebecca was still hallucinating in hospital. There was no way that Rosie was going to tell John about Suzanna and Edelberts visit, he would hit the roof. He had even got a gun to protect his family, and he was going to shoot the person he thought to be responsible for the havoc in their lives. Suzanna was going to visit Rebecca in hospital, but she was going to do it when Edelbert was on duty. Edelbert did not want the hospital to be aware that he was soliciting with his patients outside work, so he had to be very careful. Suzanna had managed to keep one of the coins from the previous exorcism attempt, and she was going to take that with her to the hospital. That following day she went to the hospital, Doctor Edelbert was on duty, she met up with him during his lunch break and they talked mainly about Rebecca. Afterwards she went to the medical ward were Rebecca was. Rebecca was still hallucinating. "Who are you? I know you," she said as she stared at Suzanna right in the eye. "My master knows you, he told me to watch out for you," she laughed. She kept laughing while Suzanna tried to talk to her, then she grabbed her by the collar. "My master is coming for you! my master is coming for you!" she yelled, that the orderly nurse came to try calm her down. She looked at the nurse, then said "You know the master is coming," she grinned. The nurse left to inform the nurse in charge so she could be given a tranquilizer. "Who is your master?" asked Suzanna. "Don't pretend you don't know him, you met with him once. He told me he knows you, and that he has got your family. We are all going to change! we are all going to change!" she yelled. Rebecca then went rigid, she looked comatosed, her eyes were wide open staring at the ceiling. Suzanna got the coin from her bag and placed it on Rebecca's stomach, that is when she started foaming from the mouth, then slugs started coming out of her mouth. Suzanna was petrified, she got her coin, then put it back in her bag, and called the nurse. When the nurse came, Suzanna left immediately, she could barely breathe. She went downstairs to the accident and emergency ward to see Doctor Edelbert. "I can't take it Edelbert, Iam leaving, I will meet you at your apartment when you finish your shift. She burst out of the hospital and left Doctor Edelbert in confusion. Whether those slugs were real or not Suzanna didn't hang around to find out, she left Rebecca with a nurse and dashed out as fast as her legs could carry her. Edelbert took it with a stride, he kept his compusure throughout the whole shift. Back at Bramwell Rosie was contemplating on contacting a medium, as long as he or she turn up while John and the boys were out. She looked in the local phone directory and she found one locally, her name was called madame Zhoux. She was an oldish lady who had always practiced alchemy and witchcraft, however she called herself a good witch. She was no more than five foot tall, had grey hair, always tied in a careless bun, and she was plump in stature, and had curious green eyes wide apart. She was of french origin. She used everything from tarot cards, candles, ouija boards and tea leaves. She claimed that she could channel the dead as well. Madame Zhoux was to arrive at Bramwell in a few days, and Rosie kept her mouth shut, she didn't tell John nor the kids about it, and neither did she tell Edelbert and Suzanna. Part of her was suspicious of Suzanna and Edelbert, she partly thought that they could be members of the cult. After his shift Doctor Edelbert took Suzanna out for dinner, they went to Hilsbury restaurant. That night the restaurant was pretty quiet, there was a few customers, they didn't recognise anybody there. It was queit enough to talk without distractions. "What happened when you were with Rebecca? what made you flee like that?" Edelbert asked Suzanna. They had just finished eating their starters, and were waiting for their main meal. They had a bottle of wine of which they were lesuirely drinking as they waited. "Remember Audrey, when those slugs were coming out her mouth, well, I saw that on Rebecca. "I didn't tell you that I kept one of the coins which we got from Father Francis, I put it on her stomach, that is when the slugs started coming out of her mouth, that is when I fled," exclaimed Suzanna. "It was bringing back memories that I would rather forget," cried Suzanna. Edelbert reached out for her hand, comforting her, "It's understandable, I can totally understand," he said. "The entity is inside of Rebecca, or communicating with her at least. She told me that her master knows me, and has been waiting for me, also that he has got my family, and that we are all going to change. What does that mean?" Suzanna exclaimed. "I don't know Suzanna, it could mean many things. I think we need to find Father Dowling he must be somewhere in some monestary, or we could find a different priest. Perhaps if we go to the vicarage where Father Francis lived, talk to a few nuns we might find a priest who will be willing to help," said Edelbert. "Ms Biggs, she was a sacrifice right," said Suzanna. "The poor woman was crucified upside down, and police still haven't found the culprit. "I believe Roger and his gang did it, they killed her as a message to anybody who dares expose their cult. I hear Ms Biggs was spending a lot of time with Rosie Lawrence from Bramwell. I think it was reason enough for them to kill her. Ms Biggs spoke a lot, and it costed her life," declared Suzanna. I heard that Mayor Jenkins and Roger are best of friends, do you think they collaborated in killing Ms Biggs," asked Suzanna. "A lot of the times they are together, and those weekly meetings they have at the village hall, I wonder what happens there," replied Edelbert. "Are you sure you want to get involved in all this," Edelbert was cross examining Suzanna. "If you want out, I can understand," he proceeded. "I don't know, but at the same time I feel for the Lawrence family. If we don't help them, they are going to end up dead. I need a day to think about it," replied Suzanna. "Okay then, it's alright then. Let's finish up here, and go home," he replied. They, finished their meal and left. Throughout the journey back to Edelberts neither of them spoke.

Chapter 4

Madam Zhoux arrived at Bramwell, it was an early afternoon, John was at work, and the boys in college, so it was just her and Rosie. She came carrying different potions, different coloured candles, an ouija board, and so foth. Rosie helped her bring that stuff in. "My husband is out, so we shan't have any disruptions. They sat in the kitchen. "Do you want a cup of tea, or coffee before we begin," asked Rosie. "Tea will be fine," answered madame Zhoux. "Tell me a little about what is happening here, so I can know roughly what I am dealing with," she asked as she sipped on her tea. Rosie was having tea as well. "Don't finish your tea because I want to read the tea leaves," she urged. Rosie didn't know where to begin, she had so much to say, but since madam Zhoux was going to be there just for one hour, she struggled to sum up everything that's been happening at Bramwell in less than an hour. "I will pay you more, if you can do two to three hours," she gasped. "Very well, my schedule is free throughout the day," replied madam Zhoux. Rosie took a sigh of relief. "I can sense a very powerful dark energy in this house, but please explain to me what has been happening. I want to get the bigger picture," said madam Zhoux. "We only been in this cottage for less than three months, but the things happening here are supernatural, my husband fails to see that, that is why he is not here. It started when we went to the local restaurant here, I noticed that the locals were behaving awkwardly towards us. It was as if they were gossiping about us, then came the noises in the cottage, the bangings on the walls and on the door. Fires coming alit on the fire places without anybody lighting them, and kitchen sink taps turning on by themselves, the whistlings and the footsteps, it goes on and on. And there was an old lady called Ms Biggs who lives locally, warning me that my family is in danger. She spoke of the cottage being haunted, and that my family is in grave danger because of the cult which is in practice here. In a nutshell, that is it," she gasped. "I feel a strong entity in this house, it is a very strong dark entity of destruction. There was a man who used to live here, a very powerful man, he died in this cottage, and his spirit is very much present here," she coughed, then swallowed hard. "He was a member of some cult, that is all I can feel right now. When we start, I will be able to tell you more," she hissed. "Don't finish drinking that tea, I want to read the leaves," she said. "I am nearly finished drinking the tea," replied Rosie. "Stop right there and give me the cup," madame Zhoux said, "and get me a saucer," she added. Rosie got up and got a saucer from one of the kitchen cabinets and gave it to her. She tipped the left over tea onto the saucer and was studying the shapes formed by the tea leaves. Madame Zhoux settled herself properly on the chair by wiggling, and shuffling her bottom about till she felt comfortable. She coughed again, then swallowed hard, she appeared petrified, her eyes looked razor sharp into Rosie's eyes. "You must leave this house at once," she choked. She started coughing more and more. Rosie got up and got her a glass of water. "I can't breathe! she said while gasping for breathe. "I need a moment to recover," she said. She drank the water and she felt better. "There is an entity that wants to devour you and your family, according to this thing, you are a sacrifice. It is wanting to complete a cycle of sacrifices so it can be reborn," said madame Zhoux. "Now we need a tour of the house," she said. "Don't forget that the reason I am here today is just a consultation, I want to have a feel about what is going on here first before I can think of a way to rid of the entity plagueing your family," said madame Zhoux. "Now let's us start with a tour of the house," she said. Of cause she being in the kitchen, they started there, then they moved on to the lounge. "I can feel very strong entities in here, more than a dozen souls are trapped in here," she said the same about the drawing room, and downstairs clockroom. "These entities are everywhere including the clockroom, they are everywhere," she emphasised. Then they went upstairs to Tobin's room, and Robert's room, the entities were highly active. In the spare room, it was the same; then they went into Rosie and John's bedroom, the entities were highly active as well. They then went into the family bathroom, madame Zhoux could hardly breathe in there, she left the bathroom very quickly. "There is a passage in this room that leads to hell," she said as she quickly shut the door behind her. The last room they went to was Rebecca's since it sat right at the end of the house, it was the biggest room in the cottage, roughly twenty by twenty two feet in size. Rosie led the way she opened the door, "I don't want to go in there, it's too dangerous," she cried. She made the sign of the cross, "Lord help us and save us," she whispered to herself. Rosie and John had not cleaned up the walls since the episode that they had with Rebecca, the bloody writings was still on the walls, and the scratchings as well. Madame Zhoux plucked up her courage and she entered the room, Rosie chose not to. She looked around, her confidence was dampened, then a swam of flies came out of the chimney, covering the whole room, she was chased outside by the flies. She fled out of the cottage, and Rosie followed her. "Did you see those flies!" she cried, "there is a demon in that room! it is controlling all the other lost souls in your cottage!" she yelled. "It is the soul of an evil man, that comes and goes!" she warned. "I am sorry Mrs Lawrence, I can't come back in your house, the entities in there are beyond my capabilities! I have to go!" she cried. "Fetch me my bag, and I shall be out of here!" exclaimed madame Zhoux. "Next time find somebody else! I can't come back here!" she expressed. She waited outside while Rosie fetched her bag and brought it outside to her. Madame Zhoux got her car keys from her bag and got in her car very fast. "Can I reach you again!" yelled Rosie. "No! find somebody else!" responded madame Zhoux as she drove off fast out of Bramwell. When Rosie got back in the house feeling helpless, she noticed a scarf on the bottom of the stairs, it was madame Zhoux's. 'She must have dropped it on her way out as she ran out of the cottage. This can be a point of contact, to make her come back here for it. I will ring her, tell her she dropped her scaff, then I will have to take it to her, then persuade her to come back. She can try other things like a ouija board, cleansing the cottage by burning sage, tarot cards perhaps,' thought Rosie. 'After all she had said that she uses all those things to help cleanse evil entities. I can't tell John that she has been here, he will hit the roof,' she thought to herself. 'Perhaps I should go see Doctor Edelbert, I will see him when I visit Rebecca, he will be on duty,' she thought. Visiting time was from 6pm to 8pm at the hospital, and her and John were to visit, if the boys wanted to go it was entirely up to them. As it turned out Robert and Tobin decided to go, they were not sure of what to expect. John came home a bit earlier than usual, and the boys were back on time, they all got ready to go to the hospital The hospital was fairly busy, after all it was a small hospital catering for a small community that sometimes there will be only four Doctors on duty rotating on different wards, from casuality unit to neo natal unit and everything else you can think of. The family got to Rebecca's ward, she was all sorts, one minute appearing comatosed, and the next pulling off her bedding, and trying to lash out on her family. She was hallucinating that one point she pulled Robert by the collar, calling him son of the devil. The nurses didn't mention anything to the family about the slugs, it was too bizzare to even mention. Before long the slugs started pouring out of her mouth again. John was in awe, he walked out of the hospital, and waited for his family in the car. Rosie called the nurse, and who in turn called the Doctor. Robert and Tobin were speechless, and in turn left the hospital to join their father in the car. In the car, in disbelief they started talking about what they had just witnessed. "Your mother is a lot stronger than I am. Let her deal with it, she is all sensitive, and such like, let her handle it," slurred John to the boys. "What was that dad? what's happening to Rebecca," asked Tobin. "Maybe the cottage is really haunted as people say. We need a priest to exorcise the place," said Robert. The Doctor who came round was Doctor Edelbert, Rosie's prayer was answered. He saw the slugs coming out of Rebecca's mouth, and got the nurses to sit her upright so that she wouldn't choke. They sat her upright, and allowed her to vomit the slugs into some container. In front of the nurses Doctor Edelbert tried to remain professional, but after they left the cubicle, he spoke of the supernatural with Rosie. Rosie told him about madame Zhoux the medium coming to the cottage, and what she said. "What are we going to do Doctor?" begged Rosie. "Medically we haven't found anything wrong with Rebecca, the problem is spiritual. If you are happy looking after her at home, I will happily discharge her. Discharging her will make it easier for me to help you at home, perhaps bringing in a priest." I am quite happy looking after her at home, and bringing a priest would be a good idea. We have got to try anything Doctor. That house is haunted Doctor, I know that now," cried Rosie. "If you are happy, I will go and write the discharge notes, and then you can take her home," said Doctor Edelbert. "Thank you Doctor," replied Rosie. Doctor Edelbert left to write the notes, while Rosie packed Rebecca's clothes, she called a nurse to help Rebecca out of bed and to escort them to the car. When Doctor Edelbert returned he said to her, "Call me if there is an emergency." he scribbled his home number on a piece of paper and gave it to Rosie. Rosie was meant to ask him how Suzanna was doing, but in the midst of all the happenings, she forgot, she only thought of it when she came out of the hospital walking towards the car. John and the boys were livid to see Rebecca walking towards the car, and Rosie holding her bag with her belongings. John got out of the car in awe. "What is going on Rosie! she is not coming home is she! You know she is not well! What did you tell that Doctor? that you can look after her! Are you out of your mind!" he yelled. "Women are stupid!" he yelled some more. "She has been discharged, but he is going to do regurlar visits, and he said we can call him anytime if we need him," said Rosie. She was biting her tongue, because she didn't want to get John going! John was too tired to cause an arguement. He said reluctantly, "Very well, but it's all on you. You know I have to work, and the boys have to be in college." Rosie smiled then helped Rebecca in the car. They hardly spoke throughout the journey back to Bramwell. When they got home, she got Rebecca to sit in the drawing room with the boys, while she fixed some supper. Rebecca didn't speak at all, and didn't respond to any conversations that Tobin and Robert tried to engage in. She kept staring at whatever took her fancy, one minute it could be Tobin, the next it could be Robert, or the piano, or the fire place. John decided to take his mind off things by going to work in his garage, whatever he was fixing. Supper was ready, Rosie made a simple dinner. They all sat at the kitchen table, hardly speaking, and Rosie had to feed Rebecca, she was still vacant.

Nevertheless she ate her dinner, and after Rosie helped her to bed. She slept in the spare room since her room was still covered with the bloody writings and symbols. "The change will do her good," uttered John; those were the only words he spoke since leaving the hospital.

In the middle of the night, they started hearing noises coming from the kitchen, it sounded like saucepans rattling, kitchen sink taps running, and whistling coming from up and down the stairs. John woke up first, and then Rosie, the boys had become accustomed to the noises that they chose to ignore them and went back to sleep. "I have just about had enough of this cottage!" yelled John. "Tomorrow I am putting Bramwell up for sell, and we are leaving!" he yelled with frustration. He got out of bed then put his slippers on and got into his dressing gown, and went downstairs to check the house. Rosie didn't bother get out of bed, she was too exhausted, she simply ignored the noises and went back to sleep. When John got downstairs, he checked the lounge and the drawing room, there was nobody there. Then he went to the kitchen, the taps were running, and he could still hear whistling sounds, he smelt the whiff of tobacco as well. "What is this?" he asked himself. "My family is moving out of here," he talked to himself. He went to the drawing room, opened the drawers of the cabinet which sat next to the piano, then he got his gun out. He had purchased the gun a couple of days before from some dealer in the village. He checked all the rooms downstairs for the second time, this time while holding a gun, and still there was nobody there. He went back upstairs, and checked on the boys, they were sound asleep, and there was no intruder in their bedrooms. Lastly he checked the spare room where Rebecca was sleeping, he opened the door, and to his surprise Rebecca wasn't in, she wasn't in the bathroom neither. He woke Rosie and the boys up. "Rebecca is gone! he shouted. "Let's split up, and try to find her. She is not in the house, she must be somewhere out there!" he shouted. "Tobin and Robert, you go search for her in the street and streets surrounding, while your mum and I look in the back garden," said John. They went out to the street, they were still dressed in their pyjamas, and Rosie in her night dress. She grabbed her dressing gown then joined John in the back garden, there was no lighting so they grabbed a couple of torches. Susie took one end of the garden while John scoured through the other end, the boys split up as well, Robert searched the streets on the left, while Tobin took the right. Tobin went as far as near the creek, close to Almer primary school, while Robert got as close to the village hall. Bramwell garden was huge, a couple of acres both in length and width, basically Rosie and John scoured through the garden. They went past the chicken coop, and right to the end of the garden, but they couldn't find her. The boys returned empty handed, and so did Rosie and John. They regrouped in the lounge. "Maybe we should call the police," suggested Tobin. "We have checked everywhere right!" said John. "Try to think of a place we haven't checked, she couldn't have gone far, not in her condition anyway," he proceeded. "What about the chicken coop, remember she was obsessing about those chickens," suggested Robert. "That is preposterous! what will she be doing in there!" aggravated John. "Who knows, maybe hiding," suggested Robert. "It was just a thought," he added. "Maybe she has gone to Ms Biggs house, maybe the clues lie there," jeered Tobin. "She has got no friends around here, and knows nobody around here except the Menderez's boys. Perhaps she is there John!" exclaimed Rosie. "You have got a point there Rosie, but we can't go knocking on their door, this time of night. We have to wait until the morning," responded John. "What about the police," suggested Tobin again. "They will come out because she is mentally unstable, and very sick," he added. "Police can't do anything for us, and they will not come out until the morning anyway," replied John in a brutal manner. "This is not a joke you know, Tobin. Your sister is missing, and she could be in grave danger," responded John. "I am going to search again in the garden, it's ever so dark out there, maybe your mum and I missed a spot," he encouraged. He got the torch again, "Anyone volunteering to come with me?" he asked. "I will come!" volunteered Tobin. "Right! let's get going! Rosie keep an eye on things here, just incase she shows up," he instructed. Tobin grabbed the other torch, and joined his father in the back garden. "Look thoroughly, incase your mother and I missed some place, it being so dark," Tobin took the left side while John took the right, but still there was no sign of her.

"How about the chicken coop!" Tobin suggested. "You are right, let's both go in there. John opened the door of the coop, and Tobin followed. All the chickens were not in the run, but inside the cabin. John entered, and in a corner he saw Rebecca. He shone his light on her, her face was covered in blood, she was holding a bloody knife in her hand. She had slaughtered a couple of the chickens. She put the knife down, then picked one of the dead chickens, and started drinking it's blood from the neck. "They are evil chickens she said, and we should never have eaten their eggs," she uttered. "This one is mine," she said as she held the dead chicken close to her chest. My master told me to do it. He said, if I drink the blood, I will become stronger like him," she uttered some more. John grabbed the chicken from her and threw it away, then he grabbed her hand, and dragged her out of the coop. "What is this nonsense you are talking about. You are coming with me in the house, and you are going to take a bath, and go to bed. Talking of this master nonsense! you are confused!" he said to her as he dragged her into the house; Tobin followed behind. Her hands, mouth, and clothes were covered in blood, and her whole body was shaking. When they entered the house, Rosie was more than relieved to see her back in one piece. She ran to her and gave her big hug, "I thought you were gone forever," she cried. "Run her a bath will you!" declared John to Rosie. Rosie went ahead and ran a bath for Rebecca, and helped her wash and dress, then brought her back downstairs where John and the boys waited. "What happened out there?" asked Rosie. She had made a hot drink for Rebecca and was helping her drink it. "We just found her there, in the chicken coop," replied John. "What about all that blood, where did it come from? Obviously she is not hurt, where did the blood come from?" asked Rosie. "She slaughtered a couple of chickens, and we found her drinking the blood," responded John in a careless manner. "I told you, she wasn't ready to be discharged, and you ignored me. Now she is your problem," he said then stomped away into the drawing room to fetch for himself a glass of brandy. He always took it straight, and that is how he will have it. "Tobin and Robert, do you want a brandy, I can fetch it for you," he asked them upon his return into the lounge. The fire was ablaze, Robert had taken it upon himself to light the fire, when his brother and father were out in the garden searching for Rebecca. "I must go and rest, it is good for me," uttered Rebecca. She wanted to go to her bedroom, and be alone. "Very well then dear, I will take you to your room," said Rosie. She helped her from the chair, and led her to the spare room. "I will keep your light on, in that case you can see clearly, and reduce the hallucinations," said Rosie. She tucked her in bed then left, leaving her bedroom door open. Rebecca slept through, John and Rosie chose not to disturb her. "She needs a lot of sleep, because right now her mind is running in over drive," exclaimed John. John and the boys were drinking brandy while sat by the fire, it helped to calm the mood of the house. Tobin and Robert ended up drinking so much that temporarily they forgot themselves, it led them wanting to go out. They decided to go knock on the Menderaz's home in search of Charles and Trevor. John and Rosie was okay with them going out. "They are going through enough, that a change of scenery will do them good," suggested John to Rosie. Rosie agreed with him, so they were allowed out. They left their parents pondering about Rebecca's situation, yet also for John and Rosie, it was a perfect time for them to talk without any disruptions. John went to the cellar to fetch a bottle of red wine for Rosie, it was the only alcohol that she drank, while he carried on drinking his brandy. They stayed in the lounge, sat in front of the fire, while the boys went next door to the Menderaz's. Robert and Tobin knocked on their door, and Justin came to answer the door. "Is Trevour and Charles in," asked Robert. "I will fetch them for you," he replied. He shut the door behind them, he didn't even bother to invite them in. He called his boys, "It's Robert and Tobin from next door. They are waiting outside for you," he shouted, then went on with his business. The boys sat on the slab that was in front of the house, and chatted for ages. It was Robert who brought up the subject of Bramwell. "Bramwell seems to be haunted, there is so many weird things happening there. We hear bangings on the walls, voices in the house, knockings on the front door and nobody being there. We have heard the kitchen tapes turning on and off by themselves, and smelt a strong smell of tobacco accompanied by whistling sounds," said Robert. "Yeh! he is right, we have had our fair share of sleepless nights. The place is haunted, and my sister Rebecca is living proof of that," Tobin interjected. "I heard your sister is unwell, and that whatever it is seems to have gotten into her brain. Is that right?" questioned Charles. "Yeh, her mind seems to be all sorts, she got out of hospital this afternoon," replied Tobin. "You might be right, the house being haunted. Long time ago when we visited grandpa Carlos, I was about eight years old, I heard dad and grandpa talking about Bramwell. They were in the study with the door shut, but I managed to eeves drop. I heard them say that sacrifices used to happen in that house, and the cottage being affiliated with some satanic cult. They mentioned a father Santos, and a few members of this community. You need to be careful, or need to move away," said Charles. "I also heard that every family that moves into that cottage gets killed as an offering to their satanic god," exclaimed Trevor. "Before we moved here, I asked dad about it, but he said that it is just a myth," added Charles. "I also heard dad and grandpa talk about a big black book, which they called the book of evil that leads to immortal life, and that grandpa was the chosen guardian of the book," Charles explained. "If that is true, then the book must be somewhere, and only grandpa knew where that book is. This is really disgusting, to think that in this day in age, there is still people delging into the occult. I can't stomach it," Tobin said. "Your father could be one of them," exclaimed Robert. "You must talk to him, and ask him about all these things because our family could be in danger," pleaded Robert. "Rebecca's room seems to be the most haunted, she is seeing things that are not there, hearing voices, and sleep walking. The other day, we woke up to find weird writings and symbols on her bedroom walls, they were painted in blood. She keeps talking of some master. That is the reason why she got hospitalised, the day time hallucinations, coupled with hearing voices. About an hour ago we found her in the chicken coop, she slaughtered a couple of chickens and was drinking their blood," said Robert. "What! that sounds crazy!" exploded Trevor. "If this is what country life is about! If so, I want to move back to the city," he exclaimed. "We must do our own research about Bramwell, and see what we can find," suggested Trevor. "How about if we meet up at the library Saturday afternoon, however if one of you find something new in between, we must share information, either over the phone or in person," Charles suggested. The boys spoke for ages mainly about Bramwell, and also about girls. Trevor was very much interested in Rebecca, he told Tobin and Robert, he wanted to date her, of cause he had to wait till she was well again.

Chapter 5

Rosie was beginning to feel worn out by the escapedes of Bramwell, she decided to pay Madam Zhoux a visit, returning the scarf was going to work as a good excuse for her to knock on her door. She came to answer the door. "What are you doing here! I told you, I don't want to have anything to do with your cottage, it's too dangerous, go find somebody else. My cat got killed a couple of days ago, it is because of you, and that haunted cottage of yours. Can't you see, it was a sign of warning from these people, whoever they are. They want me to back off, otherwise they are going to kill me, just like they did with my cat. "Tomcat was his name, and they drove a dagger through his heart; I am afraid they are going to do the same to me," she said as she held the door, blocking Rosie from entering. "They mustn't see you here, can't you see you dragging me into a lot of trouble, and they are targeting me, please go away, and never return again," she pleaded. "I only brought your scarf back, which you dropped on your visit," replied Rosie. "Can I come in, I have walked a couple of miles to come here. Perhaps a cup of tea, I would be so grateful," added Rosie. Madam Zhoux didn't know what to do, so she invited Rosie in. She took her to the lounge, were they both sat down, and started talking about Bramwell. "I will make you a cup of tea," she said, "I will not allow you to walk all the way back without taking a rest, so you are welcome to sit here till you are rested." Madame Zhoux couldn't help but worry about Rosie and her family. "How is that daughter of yours. You know, I left your house with such fear. The entity that dwells in your house is very powerful, and I can't tackle it on my own. The reason I can't tackle it is because it is not one entity we are dealing with here, they are many. All those souls trapped in that cottage, it is unbelievable, they have been sold to satan, that is why they can't leave till they are set free," continued madame Zhoux. "I feel for you, tell you what, give me time, a couple of days at least, and I will see what I can come up with. We haven't tried the ouija board, that communicates with the dead, and we haven't tried cleansing. Do you know burning sage helps with clearing the atmosphere of negative energies," she said, by that time she had regained her momentum. "In the mean time seek help elsewhere, priests, exorcists and such like. If we combine all that, you will be able to defeat that spirit that lies within your home," she added. Rosie thought of Doctor Edelbert and Suzanna. "I have changed my mind," said madam Zhoux, "I want to help you. Like Ms Biggs I have got nothing to lose, I have got no children of my own, and being my age, I have got nothing to lose," said madam Zhoux. I am going to need a couple of days to gather my thoughts, then we can try do a cleansing and communicating with the dead. That means burning sage, and using a ouija board, if it fails, that will mean, you bringing in an exorcist. Exorcisms are not my speciality," she insisted. I will contact you via phone, and tell you when I will be coming," she exclaimed. Rosie left on a good note. She decided to consult Doctor Edelbert and Suzanna, they were to come to Bramwell that following day, of cause it would have to be a time when John was out working. She rang Doctor Edelbert that afternoon, and he agreed with her, that she had to try anything that was on offer, including madam Zhoux. He reassured her that if it didn't work with madam Zhoux, she always had him and Suzanna to try and help.

 A couple of days passed, Rebecca's condition remained unchanged that John and the boys had grown accustomed to it. Madam Zhoux turned up. She came with her twig of sage, dry and ready to burn. She had made it into something that resembled a little broom, she also brought the ouija board to communicate with dead. When she arrived, John was at work, and the boys were in college, so it was just her and Rosie. In the mean time Suzanna had been busy in the library trying to find out more about the history of Bramwell. She met an old lady who had been working in the library for over thirty years, she knew everything about the village, even dating back to over fifty years ago. She was ready and willing to help, perhaps she knew too much. Her name was Sandra, Sandra Mason; she was a woman in her late sixtees, and the head librarian. The old lady dug into the archives, she found a couple of old books about Bramwell and a father Santos. All the books said, was describing Father Santos as a God fearing man, and that his ancestors were of mesopotamian origin. There was nothing really intriguing about this Father Santos, it was a dead end for Suzanna.

When madam Zhoux arrived at Bramwell, she was highly anxious, full of every anticipation. "I don't know why I am doing this, Lord protect my soul," she said as she sat herself on one of the kitchen chairs. She had brought an ouija board and and some sage. "Let's us start with communicating with the spirits, we will start with the ouija board of cause, as you know," she sighed. She pulled the ouija board from her bag, and placed it on the kitchen table. "Keep your hands tightly on the board, just the tips of your fingers, and whatever happens, keep your hands tightly on the board," she advised. She pulled out a red candle from her bag, then lit it. "The light will guide us to the home of the dead, if the light flickers or blows out, do not be afraid, it happens, just keep your concentration on the board. Do you understand what I am saying to you, if so, let us begin," she agitated. She pulled out a head bandana from her bag, and carefully wrapped it round her head, just like a gipsy would. Rosie sat directly opposite madam Zhoux, "If you are ready, just say so," said madam Zhoux. "I am ready," said Rosie in an unsteady voice. Rosie was so nervous that hives appeared on her face and neck. "Hold my hands," said madam Zhoux. Rosie held her hands, then madam Zhoux appeared as if she was in some sort of trance, then she started speaking in some strange language. She was in the trance for a good minute and a half, then she opened her eyes. She broke free from Rosie's grip. "I had to do that, so that I can gather your spiritual strength, believe you me, what we are dealing with is very powerful, so we have got be prepared. "I normally deal with minor issues but nothing like this, I can tell you that for nothing," she smiled warmly. "Are you sure you want to continue with this, because this entity could kill us both," she questioned. "I am sure, let's continue," urged Rosie. "You understand that once we start, there is no going back," stated madame Zhoux. "Yes I know," replied Rosie. "Lets put our fingers on the ouija board, and concentrate." Is there a spirit in this house, if no, knock once, and yes knock twice," she said. They heard two bangings on the kitchen door. "Who are you?" asked madame Zhoux. Their fingers started moving on the alphabet on the ouija board, it spelt Father santos. "How many of you are in this cottage?" she questioned. Their fingers moved on the alphabet spelling, 'many of us.' "What do you want?" asked madame Zhoux. Their fingers moved again spelling,'it doesn't concern you, get out of this house.' Madame Zhoux was petrified, worse of all Rosie, she got out of the trance. Rosie had remained unhypnotised. "This entity doesn't want me here, however, I will try cleansing your home, before I leave," she declared. She got her little broom of sage out of her bag, then she lit it. "We have got to fumigate every room with the smoke of sage," she said. They started off with downstairs, they started in the kitchen of cause, then the lounge, drawing room, and the cloakroom, then they went upstairs. Rosie led the way, they started in the main bedroom, then the boys bedroom, then the spare room, toilet, then lastly Rebecca's room as it lay right at the end. Again madame Zhoux hesitated to go in there," The entity is very strong in that room, but we must pluck up courage and cleanse that room. Rosie was scared, and so was madam Zhoux. "I hope you haven't painted over those writings because they are the clue to what is happening in your home Mrs Lawrence," said madame Zhoux. I can't interpret the meaning, but you must find somebody who can, so don't paint over it yet. In fact leave the room as it is so that when you bring in an expert, they would be able to feel the energy as well. Madame Zhoux opened the door, then entered, and Rosie followed behind. She started praying in some weird language. Immediately the door shut behind them, they were locked in and couldn't get out. There was a dead crow stuck on the bedroom window, with it's wings wide spread, it had a symbol on it's belly which resembled a hexagram. "Don't touch anything in this room, it might harm you," warned madam Zhoux. She lit the broom of sage, as the smoke started spreading in the room, they heard a loud cry in the room. It was a cry of a woman, "Help us," cried the woman. Madame Zhoux walked towards the fire place, she

The Offering

placed her hand on the fire place, and her hand got burnt without a fire being alit. She looked at the palm of her hand, and there was the mark of a hexagram. "Don't worry about that, the entity is trying to scare us," said madame Zhoux. She was walking around the room talking in a weird language. "The entity feeds off our fears, if you show fear, then it will make a picnic out of you, so remain strong and focused," warned madame Zhoux. Immediately madame Zhoux got thrown up in the air by the entity, and she was lavitating on the ceiling. She was screaming for help, and so was Rosie. Rosie tried opening the door but it didn't open. Then Madame Zhoux was thrown back onto the floor, the carpet then rolled itself from the floor, and there was an opening that swallowed madame Zhoux. The opening had always been there, it was a door way which one can pull up, because it had a handle. In most homes it always led to a secret passage. Madame Zhoux was gone, and Rosie was left whimpering away. She tried opening the bedroom door again, and this time it opened. She ran downstairs to call the police, but the phone wasn't working. She decided to walk to the police station to report the incident that had just happened at Bramwell. The main front door couldn't open, then she tried the back door, but she couldn't get out, she was trapped. She started hearing whispers, and tonnes of footsteps matching up and down the stairs, as well as bangings on the walls. She ran upstairs to her bedroom, jumped under the covers, and eventually she passed out. She was woken up by a loud knock on the door, God knows how long she had been out for. She ran downstairs to answer the door, much to her surprise, the door opened. It was madame Zhoux back, "Where did you go! where have you been?" asked Rosie. She was highly anxious, her hands were shaking terribly, she was trembling with fear. "I don't know what happened," replied madame Zhoux, "next thing I remember is that I found myself at the Abbey ruins, then I remembered what we were doing, so I walked back here. "What is that place anyway? Do you know? It must have some significance to this house. "It felt like this cottage chewed me up, then I got spitted out at the Abbey ruins. This entity doesn't want me here, I don't know what we going to do Mrs Lawrence. Perhaps you need some priests who do exorcisms," she declared. "Let's us re-cooperate for an hour, then we can finish the cleansing of that room," declaired madame Zhoux. They went to the kitchen to have a cup of tea, madame Zhoux was talking about the experiences that she faced in her line of work. "Never have I come across anything like this, this entity is too powerful," she said.

The hour went so fast, that in no time they went back to Rebacca's room to finish the cleansing. The door was open, then madame Zhoux lit her dried sage again, and started chanting in some weird language that Rosie couldn't understand. Big spiders started coming out of the air vent till they covered the whole room. "It is not real! keep focusing Mrs Lawrence," said madame Zhoux. The spiders went ablaze, and then they vanished. The room temperature started going up, it became so hot that they could barely breathe. Then the fire went out, and the room went from being extremely hot to extremely cold, that Rosie's fingers became numb. They started seeing icycles forming on the window ledges, the crow became frozen. Then the freezing died out, and then came a hurricane in the room, Rosie and madame Zhoux were thrown backwards and forth in that room. The carpet rolled over again, and Rosie and madame Zhoux got swallowed into the opening, and they found themselves at the Abbey ruins. They walked back to the cottage, they were covered in dust and clusters of dried leaves stuck onto their hair. Madame Zhoux was tired, "I can't do this anymore, I think you need to bring in other people because this entity is too big for me. Do you understand, we could have been killed," said madame Zhoux. "You need a priest, and when you find one, let me know, because I would want to be there as well when they attempt the exorcism or ritual to rid of this entity," she exclaimed. "If you don't mind, I have got to go now, I am extremely exhausted," she sighed. She didn't want to sit down, she wanted to leave right away. She got her bag, got her other bits and pieces and she left." Call me anytime," she said as she left Bramwell.

John came home with some bad news, he had been demoted from being a post master to being a mere cashier. It meant one thing, financial problems. He talked about it with Rosie, that is one thing he didn't need, he decided to put Bramwell up for sale. Rosie agreed with him, after all Bramwell was bringing in a lot of trouble for the family. Their plan was to sell off, and move back to the city. That following morning, Rosie rang up an agent which was very happy to sell Bramwell, which meant the ball was rolling. Selling Bramwell wasn't Rosie's priority, she had other things on her mind, like finding proper help for Rebecca. As long as she kept the cottage clean for potential buyers to view, that is all she had to do in regards to selling the property. The villagers decided to invite the Lawrence family to their weekly Saturday meetings at the village hall, John agreed to go. In a way it was a good opportunity for John and Rosie to meet the villagers and understand the very dynamics of how they ran their village. That Saturday, the Lawrences were greeted with such flattery, that they could have easily brushed away all suspicions they had of the village. There was no talk of the cult, nor of the big black book, it was just mingling. John and Rosie were left double guessing themselves, after all, they could have been imagining every ill they thought of the village..

Time passed, and Bramwell wasn't selling, there wasn't a single interest in the property. "We found this place fast, and how come noone wants to buy it," said John to Rosie. The answer to that is, the agents did not advertise the property at all, except John and Rosie were unaware of it. Some days the Lawrences were having undisturbed nights, and some days sleepless nights. Rebecca's condition remained unchanged.

The villagers met at the village hall, this time without the Lawrences, they were discussing Rebecca. "I think we have found our bride, she is ripe and sacculant, and she is twenty three. She is even dark haired and green eyed, as the prophecy says," addressed Roger to his people. "All that's left to do is to find her a groom, of Santos' bloodline, one of Justin's son," he proclaimed. "I will talk to Justin, and he will help us make it happen," Roger declared to his people. They formed a circle and started chanting in a strange language. At the end, they declared, "Hail! hail to the chosen one!" They dispersed and now the job was with Roger, to convince Justin, that the time was ripe. They had to marry on the night of the next full moon.

After the village hall meeting was over, Rebecca miraculously healed, she was her old self again, loving and bubbly. And days to come she remained well, and that forced John and Rosie to remove Bramwell off the market. Rosie remained sceptical, she still wanted to find out more about the history of Bramwell, it wasn't well for her, despite Rebecca's recovery. Rebecca grew fond of Trevor, to a point that they became inseperable, and slowly they were growing in love. The more they grew fond of each other, the more Rosie grew paranoid. John was happy again, and so was the boys, he even got his job back as the post master. He grew to be very grateful of the village community, for giving him another chance. Roger specifically grew fond of John, and in no time they developed a very strong relationship. John knew that it was all credit to Roger that he got his old job back. He owed his life and family life to Roger, and that now Rebecca had a boyfriend who was quite happy to marry her. John knew that it was Roger all along who had been spinning all that, however Rosie remained sceptical about Roger. She went to visit madame Zhoux to talk about the whole arrangement. "Doesn't it seem odd that my family went from being terrorised and to this happy clappy, and Rebecca's sudden recovery, something is off here," concerned Rosie. Madame Zhoux made a pot of fresh Tea, "Drink up dear, when you get to the bottom of your tea, save the tea so that I can do a reading. You know this don't you? We did that at your house, remember," urged madame Zhoux. Rosie drank up her tea, she drank it so fast that she couldn't wait for the reading. She left a quarter of the cup, then passed the rest to madame Zhoux. Madame zhoux got a saucer, then poured the rest of the tea in the saucer, and started the reading. Mmmm! Your life and your family's life is in grave danger," she said. "I told you this before, and there is nothing new I can tell you. They are planning on sacrificing your family. I don't have any knowledge about this cult, it is your job to find out more," she smiled in a warm manner. Madame Zhoux got up from the kitchen chair, walked up to a set of drawers, then pulled one open, then she got a broom of sage. "Here! take it," she said, "burn this in the house and it should give you some form of protection," she smiled again. Rosie took the sage, thanked madame Zhoux and went on her way. "I will keep in touch," she said, then left madame Zhoux' house. On her way back to Bramewll, Rosie realised that she was being followed by a beige pick up truck with tinted windows. She couldn't see who it was, but he was slowing down his vehicle behind her as she walked from madam Zhoux'. It was only when she turned into Bramwell that the pick up truck drove fast past her. Since Rebecca's recovery, Rosie was able to leave her home alone for a few hours, she was now going to the market place, to shops and even the library without worrying about her being alone. And sometimes Trevor would keep her company when he wasn't working. Rebecca and Trevor grew fond of each other, that their relationship was getting too serious too fast, according to Rosie.

There was happiness again in the Lawrence household. One day Rosie decided to take Rebecca with her shopping for some groceries, given there was only one main supermarket in the village, they went to Jack's supermarket. The supermarket belonged to one eyed Jack, as the villagers called him because he had one eye. Old Jack had lost his eye during a fishing trip, where the fishing hook flipped back into his eye, tearing his iris apart. His eye had to be extracted out. People in the village knew one eyed Jack to be the spy of the village, a lot of gossiping happened in his shop. He worked alone in his shop, catering for the whole village. One eyed Jack's wife had died a couple of years prior due to cholera, there was an outbreak in the village, and she had caught it so badly that it killed her and a few others. Old Jack was a widower with no family of his own, the villagers were his family as far as he was concerned, and he would do anything for the village. Rosie felt followed and watched by a group of people, she felt the stalking was covert that she wasn't able to pin point any particular persons following her, she felt the whole village was on it. Of cause she wasn't going to tell John that, he had just been won over by the villagers, he wouldn't believe her as usual. She thought of an incident that happened in the past, when they were still living in the city, Robert was in primary school and kept complaining about being bullied at school, John refused to acknowledge it, till eventually he saw it himself, Robert covered in bruises, that was the only way that led him to act. When Rosie and Rebecca got to one eyed Jack's supermarket, they were surprised to see the shop full of people. It appeared as if they were waiting for their arrival. Roger and his family were there, his wife came to greet them, mayor Jenkins and his family were there as well along many others. Mayor Jenkins approached Rosie and Rebecca, "Impeccable timing, now meet the village crew," said mayor Jenkins. There was at least twenty people in the shop, they all gathered together as if they were there for a purpose other than mere shopping. Mayor Jenkins took over from Roger, "As you all know I am the mayor of this village, nothing goes past me, I know everything about everybody here, so I want to introduce another collection of our community. This is Rosie and her daughter Rebecca, they have just moved into Bramwell, so everybody treat them well as part of our community," he declared. Rosie almost felt fluttered, but her senses got back to her. A man stood in the front, "This is Gilbert our school caretaker, I am sure you know of Almer primary school. He takes care of everything, he is a mute, but he knows how to do his job. He also does gardening for a lot of our locals. The next man then stood in front, "This is George Averson, our local butcher, he supplies all meat for the village, he is a farmer rearing cattle, sheep, goats and chickens. Make him a request and he will supply any meats you want," said the mayor. George lifted his hat, and said, "pleased to meet you ma'am. George was a scrawny looking man, wore a rough goatie beard, and seemed to be all over the place. He was in his fiftees, and constantly wore a smile on his face. He was married with four grown children. His wife was a loud mouthed villager, who always had knowledge of all the village gossip. There was also Malachi, the librarian, he had worked in the library for over forty years, that he become part of the furniture. He was short and stout, he smelled bad because he rarely washed. He was a bachelor in his late sixtees, and never been on a date with a woman, some thought he was a queer, meaning that he was into men. Last but not least on the introduction was Isabella, the school head mistress, she was the head of Almer primary school. As for secondary school the children from the village commuted to the city via bus transport. "Pleased to meet you ma'am, I hope your stay here will be good, and beneficial to the community," said Isabella. Isabella was a short plump woman, who dressed a bit rough, she wore her hair in a bun. She was in her early sixties, resembling a little dwarf with grey hair. She had sort of an abrupt personality, very traditional looking, with a mean face. The school caretaker and gardner Gilbert Sullivan walked with a limp, he was deaf and dumb, he understood very well through lip reading. He always carried bits of paper and pen, to communicate back, he could read and write. "Hire Gilbert any time and he will make a wander of your garden," stated mayor Jenkins. Malachi knew where every book was in the library, he was very much liked in the community. "Any book you want, I will get it for you ma'am," he said while grinning away. Who wouldn't be chuffed by such a reception, Rosie felt flattered, but she never lost her senses. "Everybody meet Rebecca, isn't she ripe and beautiful, she is like the princess of the village," flattured mayor Jenkins. "Everybody treat her like the princess she ought to be," he said in a joyful manner. Rebecca felt flattered, she felt a sense of belongingness, and even threw her anxieties out of the window, she felt comforted. Rebecca and Rosie left the shop with their groceries, and went back home. To their surprise Doctor Edelbert was waiting outside their cottage. He had been there, sat in his car for a good half an hour, waiting for them to show up. When they showed up, Edelbert unwound his car window. "I was worried about Rebecca, so I decided to come by and check on things," he said as he shut his car door and went and joined them at the door step. "Come on in Doc," said Rosie, as she forced the front door open. Rebecca didn't want to talk to him, so she dashed to her bedroom without excusing herself. It was good for Rosie, at least she could express her concerns to Doctor Edelbert without Rebecca's presence. "She is well now Doctor! back to her old self! and yet it concerns me so much. I should be happy right, noone gets that well so fast Doctor," she said. "I understand, believe you me, I have been there before. I was very much involved with your predecessors Suzanna's family, the Thomsons. I don't know whether she told you. Next time you see her ask her. Your family is the very reason why she came back here, she wants to help you, "Doctor Edelbert agitated. "I can't help but feel watched and followed, Doctor. I think mayor Jenkins is setting his people off to stalk me. To be honest with you Doctor, it wouldn't surprise me if he is even taping our telephone line," exerted Rosie. "Leave it with me Rosie, Suzanna and I have got a plan, to help you," responded Doctor Edelbert. Edelbert didn't stay long, he had just gone there to visit to reassure Rosie.

Edelbert and Suzanna got talking, it was mainly to find ways to help Rosie, never mind John, he was already bought into the cult's bravado.

The following morning the Lawrence family was woken up by huge noises coming from the garden. It was about six o'clock in the morning, it was Gilbert mowing the lawn. John went downstairs and into the garden. "What are you doing here! what the hell do you think you are doing!" yelled John. Do you realise it's six in the morning!" he yelled some more. Gilbert did not reply instead he made some signing language which John couldn't understand; the mower was still running, very loudly. Gilbert was a mute, so he made signs to John, of which he couldn't read. Rosie looked out from her bedroom window and saw Gilbert. "He is dumb John, and he is the local gardener," said Rosie when John came back to the bedroom. "I think mayor Jenkins send him to do our garden. Besides, he is harmless, he is a mute," conveyed Rosie. John and Rosie chose to ignore him and he carried on mowing their garden. When Gilbert was done with the mowing, he didn't knock on the door to communicate with Rosie, he simply vanished. "He has done the garden beautifully don't you think, Rosie," said John. They could only see the front garden, so they went round the back as well, all the hedges were trimmed to perfection, and the garden looked immaculate. "I can't believe, he didn't ask for payment; it left Rosie and John perplexed.

Weeks that followed, Rebecca and Trevor's relationship blossomed, and Gilbert kept coming once every week to do their gardening without asking for pay. Rosie decided to go to the mayors office to find out whether it was him who sent Gilbert. She knocked on his office door, and he came to answer the door. "Come on in Mrs Lawrence, what can I do for you?" he asked. "Take a sit, he said grinning away. Rosie sat down on one of the few chairs that were in the office. "Did you ask Gilbert to do our gardening, we are very capable you know. As you know I have got a husband, and two big boys, there was no need for it," questioned Rosie. "Don't worry Mrs Lawrence, Gilbert does gardening for a few of our villagers, especially the ones we deem special. You see Mrs Lawrence, your family is very special to the village," he added. "But he is dumb, how can you justify him not asking for pay, don't you think that is rather exploitative," she agitated. The mayor was sat comfortably in his swivel chair, rocking from side to side, smoking his pipe. He was a short, plump man, with a clear big bald patch right in the middle of his head, with short grey hairs surrounding the bald patch; he wore a long grey beard, of which he constantly fiddled with when talking to somebody. He fiddled with his beard, then said, "Gilbert was born dumb, and with a diformed leg, everybody around here treat him as special, just like we treat your family, Mrs Lawrence. Rosie had heard enough, so she left the mayors office with a feeling of misapprehension.

Throughout the weeks that followed Rosie kept having the feeling of being followed and watched, she saw the black pick up truck every now and again, and never saw who was driving it. Doctor Edelbert and Suzanna invited her for lunch one afternoon, he had a day off work, they met up at Hisbury restaurant, the beige pick up truck had been following her throughout the day. It drove past after she went inside the restaurant. They ordered a simple lunch, and started talking about Bramwell, Rosie had a lot to say. She spoke about madame Zhoux, Rebecca's automatic recovery, and her relationship with Trevor Menderaz. Suzanna was feeling apprehensive about the conversation, however if she was going to help Rosie at all, she had to start talking. She battled in her mind, then she decided to tell Rosie about what her family went through at Bramwell. It was shocking for Rosie to hear all that, that it left her feeling faithless. "We are hear to help you Rosie," said Suzanna courageously. They spoke for ages and that the plan was to find Father Dowling, and some of Father Francis' fellow priests. After their lunch, Edelbert and Suzanna dropped her just outside Bramwell a few minutes away from the cottage, she walked about five minutes, to the cottage. Gilbert was hanging around by the gate, and all she could see was a fleet of black birds flying all around Bramwell, a lot of them were petched onto the roof top, and some on the window ledges. Gilbert was flapping his arms as if imitating the birds, as she moved closer to the cottage, she noticed that the birds had devoured all her flowers and potted plants, it was just stems left, and tonnes of leaves on the ground. Gilbert kept following her, and flapping his arms, he was pointing at various areas of the graden. Rosie invited him in for the first time. 'If he can write, he will be able to communicate with me, I have got a lot of questions to ask him,' Rosie thought. They went into the kitchen, she grabbed a pen and paper and gave it to him. Rebecca was upstairs pre-occupied in her room. Gilbert smiled and started writing on the paper, every few seconds he wrote something, he raised his head, stared at Rosie then nodded. He gave the piece of paper to Rosie, it read something like,' I like you ma'am, I do the garden for you for free, he dashed out of the kitchen, through the kitchen door and went back to working in the garden, by then the birds had disappeared. He fiddled a bit in the garden then left Bramwell. Gilbert was a young man of age around twenty seven, with blonde hair, and blue eyes. He was extremely white in complexion, that one could easily mistake him for an albino. Even though he walked with a limp, he walked with pride. Often you would find him, dressed in khaki trousers and a green jumper, it is either it was his favourite clothings, or that he had very little clothes. He lived with his parents, the Parkwells. They were a couple that ran the local gardening shop, his father was a gardner as well, while his mother worked in the shop. He was an only child that his parents natured him very well. In the afternoons twice a week, he worked as a caretaker at Almer primary school.

Days that followed, Rosie kept bumping into him, especially at the grocery store, where he would carry her shopping for her, without being asked. He would limp very fast, everytime he was around Rosie, eager to please, then he would scribble on the paper, 'you are a very special family, then he would smile and hop away fast. Rosie also started spending time with Aida, her neighbour. Justin worked very long hours, and their boys worked Monday to Saturday, she was a lonely woman. Rebecca dating Trevor made them closer. Rosie knew Aida's daily routines, every Monday and Thursday mornings Aida went shopping, then she will stop by the village hall where they ran a woman's union... She even invited Rosie to the women's union, but Rosie politely declined. When Suzanna mentioned Carlos to Rosie, she knew that the Menderaz's family were part of the cult in operation.

The Offering

She needed a way to sneak into their house without being detected. Mondays and Thursdays seemed ideal to break into their cottage, and snoop around. Rosie also started a habit of inviting Gilbert into the house whenever he was doing the gardening for them. She will invite him into the kitchen, and they will have a cup of tea together, he always scribbled something on pieces of paper. Rosie went as far as showing him where the backdoor spare key was hidden, it was under a flower pot next to the kitchen backdoor. Incase she wasn't in, and he was doing the gardening, if he needed to make himself a cup of tea, or use the toilet, the key was there.

Rosie went to see madame Zhoux, she talked about the Menderaz family, she was worried about Rebecca seeing Trevor, and them being affiliated with the cult via Justin's father Carlos. She told madame Zhoux that Aida is always out every Monday and Thursday day time, and the house will be unoccupied. "You want to break into their house!" madame Zhoux questioned. "Oh no! you will not do that! What if you get caught!" she expressed. "We can break in about 9.30am because she leaves about nine o'clock in the morning to go do her shopping, Justin will be at work, and so will the boys. This is our only chance," cried Rosie. "Oh! now it's us! what makes you think I want to do that. I don't want to be arrested," responded madame Zhoux. "We won't get caught, because she practices her routine without fail. Like me she leaves the back door key under a flower pot, incase of emergency. I have been spending a lot of time with her, to know better. "Very well then," replied madame Zhoux. "Thursday it is, I will pick you up about 09.20am, then we will head straight there," she added.

Thursday came very quick for Rosie, she had been hiding that secret from her family, especially Rebecca, she didn't want Rebecca to think that she was conspiring to break her up with Trevor. She was smitten by Trevor, that she started spending some nights at his house. 'You spoil everything,' that is what Rosie imagined Rebecca saying if she found out. Rebecca was still in bed when madame Zhoux turned up at 09.15am to pick Rosie up. She parked her car at Bramwells, and they walked next door to Justin's house. There was nobody home, they went through the back way, and low and behold the back door key was beneath a flower pot. It was daisies growing in that pot and they were in season. They opened the kitchen door and they got inside the cottage. All the while madame Zhoux kept looking around to see whether there was anybody spying on them. The house was neat, and everything in order. They scoured through the kitchen, and they couldn't find anything of interest. They then went to the drawing room, and living room, there was nothing out of the ordinary. They went upstairs, and started with the main bedroom, and then the boys bedrooms, still they couldn't find anything odd. There was a spare room which was locked, maybe inside there was what they were looking for, of which they didn't know what exactly. "There must be something hidden in there," murmured Rosie. "Let's check the bathroom," said madame Zhoux, "a lot of secrets always lie hidden in the most obvious places, like the bathroom," she said. They went into the bathroom, nothing obvious was there, then madame Zhoux spotted an opening in the bathroom floor. It seemed like a secret passage. Let's open it," madame Zhoux said. Rosie bent down then opened the secret doorway, it led somewhere. "Let's go inside," asserted madame Zhoux, "I will lead the way. She opened her bag, got some sage, then lit it to sanctify the passage. There was a ladder made of rope that they used to climb down the passageway, when they got to the surface, they let go of the ladder, and started walking following the passage. It was dark and dingy through the passageway that they held hands incase they seperate. They found themselves in a tunnel, which they followed through, eventually they found themselves out of the passage. They found themselves at the Abbey ruins. "How is that possible," said madame Zhoux. "It means that you have got a similar passageway at Bramwell. Remember when I found myself at the Abbey," said madame Zhoux in a concerned manner. From the Abbey they walked back to the Menderaz', they had seen enough for the day, but they had to lock up, before Aida came back from her day's rendezvous. They locked the back door, and placed the key where it was, underneath the flower pot. They had done it without being caught. "There is still that spare room that was locked," said madame Zhoux. "I will sort that out, it takes a little bit of manipulating Aida, and then hey presto! we will be in there!" smiled Rosie. They went back to Bramwell, chatted a bit, and madame Zhoux went her way. She did not want to stay long enough for John to be back home, nor the boys.

Nearly everytime Rosie was in the village centre she kept bumping into George, Malachi, and Isabella, and would be extra flattering towards her. "When is the big day coming up, Rebecca and Trevor tying the knot," Isabella asked Rosie. "We don't know yet! I hope soon," Rosie replied.

Suzanna had been spending a lot of time in the library, reading about the history of the village, she came across a lot of information. Most of it wasn't helpful to her at all, she wanted information about Bramwell, but there was next to none. Edelbert was more interested in finding Father Dowling, but there was no leads anyway of his whereabouts. When they met up with Rosie at a secret location, they spoke of bringing in a local priest, to see whether he was able to do an exorcism, or a ritual of some sort. The three of them got together and paid a visit at the local parish. It was Father Thomas they met, who lived in a vicarage just round the corner from his church. He lived alone in a little cottage, and had a house keeper called Rosa who was a devout christian. Rosa did all the cleaning and the house work for Father Thomas. She worked from six in the morning to seven in the evening, she will be in to make breakfast for Father Thomas, and leave about seven in the evening after she had prepared supper for him. His little cottage was immaculate, it consisted of two medium sized bedrooms, a tiny kitchen, living room, and a study no bigger than seven by seven feet in size. Father Thomas smoked a pipe, so there was a very pleasant smell of tobacco. He spent most of his time in the study. He liked reading, mainly philosophy books, and he also spent a big chunk of his time preparing for his sermons. Saturdays was the day he did charity work, like working in soup kitchens to help feed the poor and the homeless. He was in his sixtees, short and plump, and bold with little hairs on either side of his huge head. He had little green eyes, and a sharp nose with flurred nostrils, one could have easily mistook him for a goblin. He welcomed the three of them, and Rosa had the kettle boiling for a nice cup of tea. He was addicted to strong tea and strong tobacco, so it wasn't surprising to see him continually smoking his pipe. He hated open fires, so often the vicarage was extremely cold, because he didn't like the fires. Underneath his brief trousers he always wore long jones, and was a big fan of thick thermal socks. He would rather double his clothings than have a blazing fire. Rumours had it that, he didn't like open fires because when he was a child his whole family, but one, perished in a fire that was started by his little brother Joe. It was an accident, but Joe survived, and he never spoke to him since. Joe lived in the village and had very little to do with his brother neither. During the accident, Joe lost his arm while struggling to escape, hence the villagers called him one armed Joe. Joe was not religious, after that incident, he never wanted to believe in God. He was a loner, who lived a life of recluse, he had a couple of dogs that he named Jack and Jill. His dogs was his family as far as he was concerned. He lived in a run down cottage close to the creek, in fact he lived a couple of doors away from the late Ms Biggs. He was an observer, and hardly joined in with the activities of the village. He had once grown fond of Ms Biggs, after her husband died of cancer. Ms Biggs and one armed Joe had become very close friends, neither of them liked the village, often they shared experiences, and secrets. Father Thomas was totally estranged from his brother, they hadn't spoken since the incidence. Suzanna, Edelbert and Rosie started talking about Bramwell, and about the escapedes happening there, and how Rosie was in desperate need of help. "Bramwell! did you say!" cooed Father Thomas. "I have got no business with that place! I can't help you! if you kindly leave!" he asserted. Neither Rosie, Edelbert, and Suzanna were willing to leave, until he heard what they had to say. He told them a story about his childhood, and how his family perished in a fire which was started by his younger brother. His brother survived and how they never spoke since. "I have always blamed my brother for that accident, and I will never forgive him for it. I felt he was brainwashed by some cult, and they made him kill his own family. Perhaps you ought to talk to him instead about Bramwell," said Father Thomas. "I am sorry, I can't help you, go to him instead, and good luck," he said. He showed them the door, and then banged the door after them. He appeared extremely worried, he matched up and down the vicarage, smoking his pipe and scratching his head till he eventually settled down. "How do we find this Joe, I remember Father Thomas saying, that he was well known in the village as one armed Joe. Maybe we should ask just random people in the village, they might be able to tell us were he lives," Suzanna exclaimed. Now they had a mission to find one armed Joe, it was exciting for both Edelbert and Suzanna.

Rosie was busy feeding the chickens and talking to Gilbert. She went back in the house using the back door, when she got into the kitchen, she found some artifact on the kitchen table. It was a cross made out of dead bits of grass and old branches, it appeared to be some form of voodoo artifact. She didn't want to touch it, she went to the drawing room to fetch John's old newspaper to handle it with. On the dresser she found a voodoo doll with pins stuck on it, the pins were mainly around the heart. She was scared, so she rang madame Zhoux immediately, for advice. Madame Zhoux was least surprised, because whatever was happening at Bramwell, it wasn't going to go away easy, the entity was growing stronger, and things were going to become worse, she warned Rosie. "Don't touch any of it! do you understand! Get rid of it! and use something to pick it up with, and burn it as soon as possible," she urged. Rosie did as she was advised, she got one of John's old newspapers from the cabinet, pulled out a couple of pages, and used them to handle the artifact and the voodoo doll, she threw them in the fire that was already ablaze in the drawing room. Rosie immediately suspected Gilbert of planting those items in her house, after all, he was the only person around. Rebecca was out, she was spending time with Aida while waiting for Trevor to finish work. Rosie called Gilbert in, and asked him whether he put those artifacts in her house. Gilbert shook his head, he grabbed a bit of paper and scribbled, 'I haven't been in the house today.' She still suspected him, so she forbad him from entering the house without her being there. She also moved the spare key from underneath the flower pot to somewhere else.

Chapter 6

Doctor Edelbert and Suzanna were to meet up with Rosie at the library, the library seemed to be a safe place for them to meet. After all Doctor Edelbert suspected that he was being stalked, and his telephone lines taped, it was unsafe. Rosie was feeling anxious, she wondered what information they had gotten. She waited for them in the library with anticipation, eventually they turned up. Susanna was wearing a blue top, and a brown skirt, and Doctor Edelbert looked smart as usual wearing a bearge suit and tie. He always dressed smartly whether be at work or on casual occassions. He was a man of integrity, and of a balanced mind. Beige was his favourite colour that more often than not he would be wearing a beige suit, and variable coloured shirts. They sat at the desk in the corner where they couldn't be distracted. There was hardly anybody in the library, as it was early in the morning. "We have got to find this one armed Joe, we might get some help from him," said Susanna. Rosie agreed, "Perhaps I could ask around, or ask Gilbert the gardner, he is mute but he can communicate using signs or in writing. Gilbert is well known in the village, and I am sure he knows a lot of people in the village as well," Rosie responded. Edelbert and Suzanna were going to ask around as well. They spoke for ages, and Rosie expressed her concerns about Rebecca being in a relationship with Justin's son Trevor. "I don't trust Carlos' family, and I feel they are using Rebecca for something involving the cult. I can feel it, and her recovery overnight, and jumping straight into a relationship with Trevor. She is spending a lot of time there, either with Trevor or with Aida, his mother," expressed Rosie. "We will dig about that as well, so don't worry," Edelbert reassured. After their talk, they went out for coffee, and from then Rosie went back home. Gilbert was busy replacing the flowers that were devoured by the black birds. Rosie had given him some money to buy new flowers and plants, his parents after all owned the garden shop, so they kindly gave Rosie a few extra plants for free. "They are a special family for the village," said Gilbert's father to Gilbert. "Behave yourself while you are there doing the garden," he perpetuated. Rosie was grateful for the extra flowers and plants, she invited Gilbert in for a cup of coffee and cake. He was delighted, all he wanted was to regain Rosie's trust. He liked Rosie, and he remained loyal. He scribbled something on a piece of paper, it read something like, 'I am not like my mother and father. They are not nice people, Mrs L.' Rosie took a sigh, she was confused by their kindness. Anyhow she asked Gilbert about one armed Joe. Gilbert knew one armed Joe and he knew where he lived. He got the piece of paper again which he had scribbled on before, and scribbled on it, 'I will show you where he lives tomorrow afternoon.' "Very well," said Rosie, "tomorrow it is," she replied. After the coffee, Gilbert went back to his gardening, he even cleaned out the chicken coop, and he refused payment from Rosie. "I am doing this for free, because you are a nice person," he conveyed in sign language, then he hopped away. Rosie was still puzzled about the artifacts, if Gilbert didn't plant them in the house, then who did? She put the thoughts away and concentrated on meeting one armed Joe. She was going to go without Suzanna and Edelbert, to meet this Joe, she couldn't wait. Next afternoon Gilbert was eargely waiting to show Rosie where one armed Joe lived. They set off, with Gilbert hopping along, they walked passed the creek, and past Almer primary school. Right opposite Ms Biggs house was were one armed Joe lived. He welcomed them, and immediately he recognised Gilbert, he hadn't seen him in years. He was very welcoming, considering he was a recluse. The minute they were made welcome, Rosie dismissed Gilbert. "You can go now, I will meet you back at Bramwell," said Rosie politely. Gilbert left, he hopped all the way back to Bramwell. One armed Joe was intrigued by the visit, he never got visitors except for Ms Biggs when she was still alive. "What brings you?" asked Joe. "Please sit down, it must be something important," he smiled. Rosie sat down, on a half broken settee in the living room. One armed Joe's house was dark and dingy, there was barely any furniture in it, it looked very eccentric like the owner. Joe was a scrawny looking man, in his early sixties. He was about six foot four, thin and bony, he wore a rough looking grey stubble, with long grey hair which looked unkept. There was a strange smell in his house, perhaps a mixture of stale tobacco and stale clothings, and mould. The house was damp, and mouldy. He lived like a beggar, living off very little, and budgeting on whatever little he had. Rosie felt a bit apprehensive, she didn't know whether to stay or run for it, but still she was there for a purpose and that is what she was going to stick around for. "Did you know Ms Biggs, you see, I was a good friend of hers, and her death still puzzles me. And I wonder if you know anything at all about who might have killed her," asked Rosie. One armed Joe was a chain smoker, he smoked rollies. He got his tobacco from an old chest of drawers that looked like it was going to fall apart. He sat himself down then rolled a cigarette, got a box of match sticks and lit it, and started puffing away before he could speak to Rosie. "I knew Ms Biggs, she was my one and only friend in this village. She was murdered by the villagers, perhaps you should ask the Mayor, who killed her, and maybe Roger might help as well," he smirked. Rosie struggled hard to make herself comfortable in that half broken settee, she wriggled and jiggled till she found herself a comfortable position. "I live at Bramwell cottage, is there anything you can tell me about Bramwell. I met your brother you know, a Father Thomas, he didn't have any nice words to say about you," Rosie was enquisitive. Joe took a puff of his cigarette, then smirked. "You see Mrs Lawrence, my brother and I don't get along at all, he disowned me when I was a kid, I was about fifteen, and we haven't spoken since. Some people in the village took me on, after the fire killed our family. The fire killed our father and mother, two sisters and two brothers younger brothers of cause. I started the fire, that is why Thomas became a priest and disowned me, because I started the fire," he paused a bit. "Do you want a cup of tea or coffee?" asked Joe. Rosie was feeling uncomfortable, "Tea will be fine," she replied hesitantly. Joe got up and went to his grubby kitchen, and made two cups of tea, he came back, and rolled himself another cigarette. Even the tea stunk of tobacco, Rosie was a bit

The Offering

apprehensive about drinking from one of his cups, his hygiene was highly questionable. She drank it nevertheless out of politeness. "Did you say you live at Bramwell? he questioned. He immediately felt nervous. "Yes we bought Bramwell, and moved in not long ago," responded Rosie. Joe took a few puffs of his cigarette, and coughed for a long while, his lungs were weak because of too much smoking. "Mmmm, that is scary, it brings back bad memories, my family lived in that house, we had moved from the city because of dad's work, and strange things started happening there." He became agitated. "I caused that fire, I caused that fire!" he shouted in an agressive manner. Rosie was scared, but she kept her nerves under wraps. He was puffing his cigarette rapidly, pacing up and down, scratching his head. "I caused that fire," he said, crying his eyes out. He went to a corner, and curled up like a lost little boy, crying away. "I didn't know what I was doing! but he still blames me for it!" he sobbed. "Ms Biggs understood me, she knew everything!" he sobbed. Rosie thought of reaching out to him, to give him a cuddle, but she was to scared of what he might do to her. "It's not your fault!" she exclaimed. "If it's any consolation, my family is going through similar stuff that your family went through. That is why I am here, to see if you can help us, before someone gets hurt, "Rosie comforted. He got up from the corner, and regained his sense of self. "Roger, and the Mayor know everything, but they are quite happy to see me ostracized by this community. Ms Biggs was the only one who was kind to me," he sobbed some more. "The Mayor's parents were part of the cult, and so was Rogers family. Roger and the Mayor grew up brainwashed by their parents, that they continued running the cult after their parents died," continued Joe. The cult is believed to have been started over 150 years ago by a father Santos, he was of mesopotamian descent, and he adopted one of his cults into the village. It is a cult that worships the serpent god, and sacrifices people, rarely animals, except a serpent of cause. My brother Thomas thinks that I was working with the cult members, and they made me murder my own family. I can't deny that the cult was responsible for my parents death and my siblings. I was just a kid, I have got memories of them taking me to the Abbey ruins were they were practising rituals. I remember them sacrificing a baby at the old alter of the Abbey. They slaughtered a baby that had been reported abducted. They slit its throat, and they made me drink the blood, I was fourteen then. They regularly threatened me, saying that if I didn't attend, they would kill me, so I complied. I caused the fire, but I have got no memory of it, except what Thomas told me. He called me the devil. He has got memories of watching me start the fire, and me locking the family inside the cottage, and fleeing. He escaped through his bedroom window, and onto the roof. I have got vivid memories of me fleeing the scene, but my left arm was damaged, that is how I ended up losing my arm. I was taken in by Roger's parents, but my brother Thomas fled and joined the priesthood at some monestary, only to come back as a priest. I stayed with Roger'sfamily for about four years, then I went off on my own, and strived to survive. The day I left Roger's family, the village made me an outcast, and I have been ever since. I don't talk to any of them, and I don't attend any of their gatherings. I learnt from Roger's parents that the cult's soul purpose was to bring father Santos back to life, and all the sacrificed people. They call it, the anticipated day of the return of the dead. It is about eternal life. They believe Father Santos is an immortal god, and can bring eternal life to all members of the cult, hence the sacrifices. There is a big black book that belonged to Santos, they call it the book of the dead, and it is somewhere in the village. All the secrets lie in that book. Find the book and destroy it," said Joe. He took a long sigh, then rolled another cigarette, lit it, took a few puffs, then continued. "Your family is not safe in that house, it was Santos' home, and many believe it is still his home," he added. Rosie was flabbergasted, she couldn't take anymore of it. "I don't know any family that has ever escaped distruction in that cottage, many have died," he warned. "Get your family out of there fast," he insisted. Rosie felt uneasy, she fiddled on the sofa, then said, "Thank you Joe, you are a nice person, you don't deserve living the way you are. You have told me what I need to know, if you think of anything else, don't hesitate to drop by the cottage. I know it will bring back horrible memories, but do it for my family's sake," agitated Rosie. Rosie didn't want to stay any longer, besides time was moving on, and she had to be back home before

John finished work. She left Joe's with a feeling of disenchantment and feeling hopeless. She walked all the way back, thinking about what Joe had just told her. When she got home Gilbert was still working in the garden, he was nearly finishing planting all the flowers and plants, replacing the ones that had been devoured by the birds.

Chapter 7

Roger lived very well, he was a wealthy man, who owned a few properties in the village. Prior to her death, Ms Biggs had gone to see a lawyer about amending her will, since Joe was her one and only friend, she left her house to him and everything else that she owned. She felt it would give him an opportunity to start a new life elsewhere, after selling the property of cause. One armed Joe had no knowledge of it, because the villagers quashed any of that knowledge ever reaching him. They bribed the lawyer who in turn destroyed Ms Biggs will. Roger wasn't going to buy the cottage, he was going to take it. Lawyer Thomkinson was too afraid to say anything, so he went along with it, and Roger became the new owner of the cottage. Roger lived in a mansion with twelve bedrooms, three reception rooms, and a couple of drawing rooms. He had three servants who served him and his wife and kids, hand and foot. He was abusive to his maids and gardner, and barely paid them. He intimidated them to a point where they were afraid to ask for their pay. They couldn't run away neither, because he would find them, nearly everybody in the village knew Roger and was somewhat controlled by him. As time went on Roger be-friended John, and before long they were spending a lot of time together at the public house. John also grew fond of Justin, and Mayor Jenkins. The four of them even went golfing together, they became inseparable. John was loving the fact that his daughter was seeing Trevor, he even took Bramwell off the market, and started spending less and less time with Rosie. He was walking in after work, only to go out again till very late, spending time with Roger, Justin and Mayor Jenkins. Rosie was feeling isolated in the house, Rebecca was always next door, and the boys with their friends, she felt alone in that cottage. 'The family was getting divided,' she thought. John started drinking more and more, before he only drank alcohol on a weekend, but with Roger, Justin, and Mayor Jenkins it became an everyday thing. The whole family seemed happy and jolly all the time except for Rosie. One night when they were out at the public house, Roger turned the conversation onto Rebecca and Trevor. "I have just purchased the old lady's cottage, the late Ms Biggs. I was thinking maybe it is time for Rebecca and Trevor to have their own place, I will give them a discount for the rent!" he boasted. Justin was in agreement, "That's a splendid idea," he said, as he galloped down his scotch; dry that is how he always took it. John was in agreement, he started a habit of agreeing with whatever Roger, Justin and Mayor Jenkins, said. Rebecca was well, and everybody was getting along with everybody, so there was no problem, in his eyes. When he got home, he told the idea to Rebecca, not Rosie; Rebecca was ecstatic. "Thank you father!" she said, "that is the most splendid gift ever!" she exclaimed as she gave her father a big hug. Rosie wasn't happy, she knew she couldn't talk John out of the idea. Roger went on to have Ms Biggs furniture removed from her cottage, he sold most of it, and the rest he put in storage. Trevor was to rent the place from Roger.

Days that followed, Rebecca was packing her stuff, and soon enough, she was co-habitating with Trevor, and Rosie couldn't do anything about it. The villagers were astounded. "It is happening," said George the butcher to Malachi the librarian, and Isabella the head mistress of Almer primary school. They had bumped into each other at the local supermarket owned by one eyed Jack. Village talks were constantly happening in that shop in a subtle manner, it was a regular meeting place for the cult members, yet undetectable. They would pose like regular customers, but communicate their plans in that shop. Rosie felt that the whole village was on it, and yet John felt like the villagers were the nicest people he has ever come across. The villagers wanted every member of the village to be involved in the cult, "Why don't they try it out, they might like it," one cult member said referring to the Lawrences. To some villagers, learning that the cult sacrificed babies, made their stomachs turn, and they would not get involved. There was a small number that kept themselves to themselves, and never spoke of the cult, that was plaguing the village.

Rosie met up again with Doctor Edelbert and Suzanna, she told them that she found one armed Joe, and had been to his place. She told them what Joe had said to her. "It's time we meet this one armed Joe," said Edelbert looking at Suzanna. "You said, he mentioned a big black book. That book perished during the ritual at the Abbey, unless if there is another one," exclaimed Edelbert. Little did he know, that the book reappeared after him, Suzanna, and Father Dowling left the Abbey, and that Roger took it. "There must be another one then, that is why the entity is still manifesting itself in Bramwell again," Suzanna exclaimed. "We must find that book, and destroy it. It must be in Rogers house because he is the one running all this," expressed Edelbert. "These last few days, I have felt that I am being watched and followed by the villagers. I feel followed when I go to work, and I feel followed when I finish work. I also feel that my phone line has been taped, otherwise how would they know about my whereabouts during the day," he perpetuated. "It is Roger behind all this." added Edelbert. Suzanna didn't feel followed nor watched, "Maybe they don't fear me," she ejaculated. "The good thing is, nobody saw me go to one armed Joes, if they did they would have surely made it known to me," said Rosie. "One armed Joe told me that, the book of the dead, is about bringing back the dead to life, starting with Father Santos, and then the rest of his disciples who were sacrificed. The ones who were sacrificed will serve the purpose for Santos' cause. They will never be who they were before, but instead be, Santos' disciples, that includes your family, Suzanna," said Rosie regretably. "I fear for my daughter, having moved in with Carlos' grandson; Carlos was one of Santos' followers, having guarded that book for many years," Rosie continued, she started crying her eyes out, and Edelbert was there to comfort her. "Fear not, your daughter will guide us, to what they are planning on doing next. The three of us will keep a close eye on her, and feed each other whatever information we get," comforted Edelbert. He reached out to her, and gave her a hug, while Suzanna held her hand. "I can't even count on John, John is already bought into this fake niceness of Roger, Mayor Jenkins, and Justin. They are the real kingpins of this cult. The boys, well, they are too absorbed in their own lives, to care," whimpered Rosie. "I am all alone now in that cottage. John even took the cottage off the market, because he is getting on so well now with those three," she continued while sobbing away. "There! there! Mrs Lawrence! we are here to help you! and we are going to try our best to help you, and hopefully destroy this entity, once and for all!" responded Edelbert. "We are going to do some more digging about this Trevor," reassured Doctor Edelbert to Rosie.

When Suzanna and Edelbert turned up at one arm Joe's place, he wasn't very reciprocative, he was suspicious of them, he thought Roger had sent them to spy on him. "We are friends of Rosie Lawrence," they said at his doorstep. He wasn't willing to let them in unless he was sure that they meant no harm to him. "We were also friends of Ms Biggs," said Suzanna. When Suzanna mentioned Ms Biggs, Joe let them in, he knew that he could trust them. He made them welcome and they sat in his filthy lounge. There was papers everywhere, alongside any bits and pieces you can think of. He made them coffee, and they started chatting. He told them everything, he had told Rosie except about the book. "What do you know about the big black book?" questioned Edelbert. "Well," Joe scratched his head while rolling himself a cigarette. "The book has been passed on generation to generation between Carlos' family and Roger's family, if it should be anywhere, it is bound to be with either one of them two families. My money is, it's with Carlos' family, never Roger's. You see, Roger talks too much, and he is too involved in the village, I believe he is just a stooge being used by the real cult leader, who is Mayor Jenkins. Roger works for Mayor Jenkins, and Carlos' family. They will never entrust him with the book, it would be too risky. Old Jimmy is one of their trustees, he does all the spying for them. Mayor Jenkins would rather trust old Jimmy, than Roger," gasped one armed Joe. "When Roger's family put me up, when I was a teenager, I managed to get hold of the big black book, it was by shear accident. Roger's father had retrieved the book from somewhere, and had left it lying around carelessly. I happened to go in his study, and there it was, lying on his desk. The cover was shimmering black with gold writing on it, and I couldn't help but be drawn to the book. I went to the desk, got the book, and started reading it. My memories from childhood are a bit hazy, but there is things that I read in there that stayed with me forever. It was called the book of the dead. I remember flipping through the pages, nobody was home, so I had all the time in the world to read through some chapters. One chapter mentioned the day of the she serpent godess. She was to come from an unknown family, and she will be twenty three years old, and dark haired, and she was to marry an heir of one of the cult followers. On that day of the full moon, they shall marry, and she will be sacrificed together with her groom, to mark the return of 'the one.' Then the chosen one shall return together with the dead who were sacrificed for the cause, and they shall rule the cult for eternity," said Joe. "The rest I can't really remember. My brother Thomas, thinks that I am the devil, that is why he disowned me," cried one armed Joe. "Thank you for sharing that with us, and remember, you are not a bad person. They brainwashed you when you were a kid, and they made you murder your family. We like you, and we want you to help us destroy this entity, and cult," responded Doctor Edelbert. Rebecca reached out and gave Joe a hug, "Don't worry, we will make sure we look after you," she expressed.

As John got closer and closer to Justin; Roger, and Mayor Jenkins, they trusted him more and more with their secrets. John started attending their weekly meetings at the village hall, and slowly he was being drawn into the cult. Justin started using brainwashing techniques on him, that John was bought into the idea of the cult. Justin never told John that John's family had been chosen to be sacrificed. John was too blind to see, and was too absorbed in the niceties of the community. He never even thought about Rosie's feelings, he hardly thought of her. His loyalty was with Roger; Justin, and Mayor Jenkins. Rosie felt like she was the hat that hung on a hat stand in her cottage, only taken off the stand to be worn, and only to be put back again. The boys started noticing a change in their mother, after Rebecca moved out. Robert was highly concerned. "Mum is unhappy, and yet all of us are happy, that is not right," he said to Tobin. "She is our mother, and she has been a very good mother, including being good to dad, perhaps we should talk to her, and see what is eating her up," continued Robert. The talk never happened, the family was now too divided to be salvaged by just mere dialogue, it needed more than that.

John started attending the weekly meetings at the village hall without fail, slowly slowly he was getting indoctrinated, and brainwashed by Roger and his followers. He even started attending their monthly ritual meetings at the Abbey ruins. One night Roger turned up at Bramwell to pick John up for the monthly meeting at the ruins, Rosie decided to spy on them. The boys were busy with the Menderaz's boys, and she was going to be home alone. She sneaked out, and followed John and Roger to the abbey ruins. She hid behind a bush right outside the Abbey entrance. There was at least two dozen of them dressed in black robes, except for John. They gathered in a circle right in the middle of the temple, a female surfaced, carrying some artifact, and then she handed it over to Roger, who in turn handed it over to John. John took the artifact, as they carried on chanting in some strange language. They started dancing around John, slowly drawing him to the centre. John appeared hypnotised, he went along with everything. The female who turned out to be Isabella, the headmistress of Almer primary school, there disguised in a robe and hood, brought in a chicken, obviously from John's chicken coop. She handed the chicken, to the leader who was dressed in a red robe. Rosie couldn't figure out exactly who it was, because his face was kept hidden from the reflection. All she could see, was the red robe, and the rest the moonlight couldn't reveal his face. Isabella then drew a dagger from one of her pockets, it was a rustic looking, black dagger, then she slit the throat of the chicken. The head dressed in red robe collected the blood in a chalice, then lifted the chalice up, while the rest danced around chanting. When the chalice was full, there was total silence; the leader handed the chalice over to Isabella, who in turn handed it over to John to drink from. He took the chalice and then drank from it, without anyone of them prompting him. "You are one of us!" they all shouted, and danced around him. They took him to the alter where the head was waiting; he knelt down, while the leader poured the rest of the blood over his head. John did not react a bit. Rosie witnessed all this. Afterwards they held a celebration, which they called the initiation, that is when

Rosie left and went back to Bramwell. At least she now knew what she was fighting against. Not only was she fighting the cult, she was also fighting John.

After the intiation, the cult members got so drunk in celebration, that by the time John got home, he had no idea what he had just done. Rosie was still awake, but she chose to ignore him. She didn't bother wake up early to prepare breakfast for John and the boys before their day started at work, and college, they had to fend for themselves, it was tough for them. 'How can they not understand, where I am coming from?' she asked herself. They had woken up with their bodies covered in strange markings. It was John who first noticed, he saw the markings of strange writings on his body, and he chose to ignore it, and carried on as if nothing had happened, he left for work, and he was happy as before. Tobin and Robert noticed the same markings, they were concerned that they started talking about it between themselves. "Dude, I woke up with these marks on my body," said Tobin to Robert. Robert looked at the marks, they looked like tattooes. He then took his T shirt off to check on his body, only to find he had similar markings on his body too, they were both puzzled. "Maybe mum is not that crazy after all, when she rumbles on about some entity dwelling in this cottage. What does that mean. I guess after college, we need to dig into this nonsense of mum's," said Robert. They didn't think much of it, at the time, they got theirselves ready while Rosie had a lie in. When she woke up, she found the markings on her body too, she wasn't shocked anymore, anything was possible and believable. The house was empty, it gave her time and space to think. While she was thinking, she thought of turning Rebecca's room into a sewing room. She was going to be busy moving all her sewing stuff from her bedroom to Rebecca's room. She worked so hard most part of the morning that by midday she had finished. 'I have to think about myself from now on, and please me, so I am going to be spending most part of my days sewing in the sewing room,' she thought. John was actually pleased with her efforts, he praised her for it. "It's good that you are getting a life," he said. "I am only doing this, because none of you believe me, when I say this cottage is dangerous for the family. You all act out like you are happy," she expressed. John paced up and down as if agitated. "But we are all happy except you. You just don't want to admit that there is nothing wrong with this village," he agitated. "One day, I will prove you wrong," replied Rosie. "Why don't you start off by taking your shirt off. I want to see the markings on your body. You can't do that can you!" "Your sons showed the same markings on their bodies before they left for college this morning, I was half asleep you see so I heard everything," she asserted. "John! I have got the same markings as well! they look like hexagrams! do you understand anything about witchcraft! or the people you are choosing to associate yourself with! You haven't got a clue have you!" she scolded. "It's all in your head! you need to see a shrink!" he yelled. "I have got to be out with Roger, Justin, and Mayor Jenkins, and you are trying to spoil it for me! that's what it is!" he yelled some more.

The ceremony at the Abbey ruins was to last a week, according to Roger, John had to attend everyday of that. The second day of the ceremony Rosie got in touch with Suzanna and Doctor Edelbert, to share with them the information about the ceremony. Edelbert and Suzanna were able to spy on John and the cult members throughout the whole week. They would hide behind the bushes by the ruins entrance, and were able to watch everything happening there.

Rosie's markings never went away, and she presumed it was the same for John, Tobin, and Robert. She wondered whether Rebecca had the same markings. Everytime she tried having a quiet word with Rebecca, Justin was always there at Trevors. She hardly visited Bramwell, because she was too absorbed with Trevor, and his family. If anybody could have explanation for the markings, it would be one armed Joe, because he once lived in Bramwell. She paid him a visit, he was always home, he didn't have a job. One armed Joe bought his little cottage from proceeds that came from his dead parents, he survived on very little, and often from the help of the late Ms Biggs. When Rosie got to his cottage, he was least surprised to see her there. "I knew you would come back, it looks like I am the only friend you have got," he said grinning away. Rosie sat herself down, and they started talking. "Do you know Ms Biggs left me her house, and everything else that was in there, but Roger took it," he said in a very calm tone. "He controls everybody in this town, including Lawyers. Ms Biggs told me a few years ago, that she was leaving the house to me and that If I was lucky I would sell it, and move away," added Joe. "But Roger took it, does it surprise you?" he asked. "Nothing surprises me here, imagined or unimagined," responded Rosie. "I have got markings on my body that came from nowhere, and so does my family. We all got hexagram markings; what does that mean?" she asked. "These cult members hex people, it means that your family has been marked for death, for sacrifice. My family went through the same thing, while we lived at Bramwell. You need some help, if you want to save your family. These people are powerful. I am not even going to fight Roger over Ms Biggs' house, because I will lose, or end up dead," declared Joe. "Thomas is a priest, he should be able to help you, he knows everything there is to know about rituals, and exorcisms," added Joe, he was smoking away. "Your daughter is under a trance, you can never get through to her; you have got to do something," urged Joe.

Days that followed were full of anguish for Rosie, she met up again with Doctor Edelbert and Suzanna, and news had gone round the village that one armed Joe was found dead in his cottage. Heart attack is what the Doctor called it. 'How convenient is that for Roger,' thought Rosie. Rosie, Doctor Edelbert, and Suzanna attended Joe's funeral, Father Thomas was nowhere in sight. 'Good riddance,' he said to himself. Even in death, Thomas couldn't find it in his heart to forgive his brother for the fire he caused that killed the rest of their family. Roger had nothing to fear now in regards to taking the late Ms Biggs property.

The year of the full moon and return of the godess was approaching, the cult members were excited about sacrificing Rebecca. Roger had murdered one armed Joe buy poisoning his food, he wasn't going to have Joe tattle telling to Rosie about the cults secrets. Joe had loved Gilbert, besides Mrs Biggs, Gilbert was the only other person Joe had trusted, but Roger had manipulated Gilbert to poisoning Joe. After Joe's funeral, Rosie got home to find Gilbert inside the house; how did he get in there? She caught him by surprise, he was in Rebecca's old room. The room was trashed, everything turned upside down, he was searching for something. He was looking for a key, the key was very important to him. "What are you doing in my house!" Rosie yelled at him. He appeared extremely nervous, "I was looking for something," he signed hesitantly. He pushed Rosie aside, and left Bramwell. He created such a big mess, that it took Rosie all afternoon to sort that room up. While Rosie was away at the funeral, Gilbert had scoured everywhere in the back garden to find the back door key. He had found it in the bottom of the hanging basket by the kitchen door step, and gotten himself in. ' Who is he working for?' Rosie questioned herself. 'It has to be Roger,' she answered herself. Rosie remembered Suzanna talking about some key, the key was still there somewhere in Bramwell. She searched everywhere in the house for this particular key, but to no avail. As she searched her bedroom drawers, she found a dagger hidden underneath John's socks. It was his own set of drawers for his underpants and socks. The dagger was about a foot long, silver in colour, and had strange inscriptions on the side. She picked it up, took a good look, then placed it back in the drawers. She wasn't going to say anything to John, she didn't trust him anymore. She tidied up the whole house, and started thinking of what could been going on. That afternoon she went to visit Father Thomas again, she was curious as to why he did not bother attend his brother's funeral. She got to the vicarage, he was in, and he allowed her in. "I know why you are hear Mrs Lawrence, and you know what answers you are looking for. So why are you here, when you know already?" questioned Father Thomas. "They killed him, you know that. What do you want from me, you know I can't help you," he agitated. "I can't mourn for my brother, you know that. What do you want from me, and whatever it is, I can't help you," he insisted. "I feel safe in the church, and I suggest you seek the church as well," he urged. "They took the house left for him by Ms Biggs, and he died for it, this is how they operate. Mrs Lawrence take your family out of this village, and return to the city at once," he warned. "I believe Joe told you everything you need to know, and I am not going to repeat it. You are a smart woman, and you know that, so if you kindly leave me alone, I will be so grateful," he said as he led her to the door. Rosie had to do something to save her family. If she learnt anything, it was that, this cult was controlling the whole village. 'But Father Thomas could at least help, with some exorcism or ritual at least,' she thought. She wasn't done with him. She left, and she contacted Doctor Edelbert and Suzanna, and after all, there was also madame Zhoux. Madame Zhoux wanted to know what was going on as well.

Rosie didn't dare ask John about the dagger she found in his sock drawers, he was now totally under the trance of the cult. She simply left the dagger there,' what was it for,' she asked herself. Rosie thought that the cult murdered one armed Joe, not because of Ms Biggs house, but because he was seen talking to Doctor Edelbert and Suzanna, and also that she must have been seen going to his house. They couldn't have him going round tattle telling about their cult. 'It all started in Rebecca's room, there must be something in there, perhaps a clue or something,' thought Rosie, she decided to spend one whole morning searching in that room, she was going to search with a fine toothed comb. John and the boys were out, she made some strong coffee for herself, to help her stay alert. She started by the door step, literally studying the door, then moved on to the walls, she started ripping off the wall paper. After ripping the wall paper by the bed headboard, she found a revelation, there was a little door, it appeared as if it was a safe, there was a key hall, and the little door was locked. 'There must be a key somewhere,' she thought. She removed all the wall paper in the room, but there was nothing else. She thought of the safe, then she went downstairs to John's garage to find some screwdrivers, per chance she could be able to open the safe. She got a couple of small screwdrivers, and tried to open it, but she couldn't. After she thought she was done scouring through the room, she looked at the fire place. 'Maybe there is something up that chimney,' she thought. As she got closer to the fireplace, a swam of black bats flew out, they were so many that they nearly blinded her of visibilty. She ran out of the room, the bats chased her out of the cottage then they flew away. Rosie wasn't scared, by now she had gotten accustomed to the strange happenings in the cottage. She went back to the room, this time with more determination than ever. Whatever was going to happen, she was going to keep John out of that room. If he were to learn that Rosie had removed the wall paper, he was going to hit the roof with fury, so she was going to keep that her secret. Neither Toby, nor Robert was ever interested in going in that room anyway. She got to the fire fireplace, looked around but there was nothing to be found, then she looked up the chimney, there was nothing there. She went downstairs to the kitchen to fetch a broom, then she started sweeping the chimney. As she fiddled with the broom up the chimney, touching every corner, down came a crow, it was dead, stiff as a broom, it had it's wings spread out. It had its toes cut off, and there was markings of a heaxagram on its body, on the stomach area, the eyes had been pocked out. The markings were burnt markings. She picked the crow up, took it to the back garden to burn it. She poured kerosine on it and she set it on fire. As it was burning, the chickens in the coop became restless and they were cooing so loud that almost deafened her. The crow burnt till there was nothing left. After it burnt down, the chickens stopped cooing. After all that, Rosie felt extremely tired, she felt as if life had been sucked out of her, that she nearly passed out. That is when she decided to take a nap. She was out for the couch, till she was woken up by Tobin and Robert, it was nearly dinner time, and there was no supper prepared. She made supper for the family, and as usual John came in very late, just to eat and sleep. As she was getting herself ready for bed, John was in the drawing room, as she passed the drawing room, she heard him having conversation with someone over the phone, she assumed it was Roger. It was Mayor Jenkins on the other line, "When is the day of the sacrifice, so that I will make sure she is in," that is what she heard John say. She stood by the door, then listened some more. They were speaking about the Abbey ruins, and the silver dagger. Rosie heard that, after John got off the phone and came to bed, Rosie pretended as if nothing was happening. She lay in bed thinking, and hardly slept, while John snored away.

Chapter 8

Rosie kept bumping into Gilbert everytime she was in the village centre to get some groceries. He kept offering her help carrying her groceries, but she kept refusing his help, he was relentless with his persuit, but she kept adamant that she didn't require his help. As much as she kept bumping into Gilbert, she also kept encountering Isabella, George and Malachi, they were all trying hard to force conversation with her, but she kept running away from them. "Sorry I have got go," was her regular excuse. The other thing on her mind was to invite Rebecca home for the weekend, without Trevor. She was curious to know how things were going for her. The thought of Ms Biggs, and how she died, kept haunting her, and the thought that her daughter was living in her house, and that one armed Joe died for that house, unsettled her. She wanted Rebecca back at Bramwell, but John was never going to allow that. 'What was it with the markings on their bodies anyway, and whether Rebecca had them as well,' she pondered. Then she remembered Father Thomas warning her that they were hexes, in other words, they were marked for death, to be sacrificed. They had markings of hexagrams, which were not going away, how they got there they didn't know.

Rosie went to see madame Zhoux, she told her of her new discoveries, she spoke of the secret safe which, was hidden behind the wall paper. Madame Zhoux was curious that they went back together to Bramwell, so she could see for herself. They could not find a way to open the safe, she stood infront of the safe, meditating to channel some sensation. After the trance, she told Rosie that there was a book, in the safe, more like a diary, that would explain a lot about the cult. "I am sensing the diary belonged to the cult leader, and in the diary, is written every step by step of the order," she exclaimed.

"Someone knows where the key is, but I can't pick up who," she exclaimed. From then, they pulled off the carpet, opened the passage doorway, and there was a stairway leading deep into the ground. Madame Zhoux got her sage, lit it up inorder to purify and neutralise the entity, if she didn't do that, danger could befall them as they climbed down, and walk through the passageway. Rosie had a torch ready, and followed madame Zhoux down the steep steps. As they walked through the tunnel, they were hearing voices, and chantings. "Ignore all that," said madame Zhoux. "The voices are meant to scare us away, keep walking, and follow me behind," she insisted. It was a long tunnel, about one third of a mile, and had different passageways leading to the main. Presumably one of the passageways must have led to Justin's house. The tunnel was extremely dark, and eeiry, but madame Zhoux persevered onwards following the main passage, that is something Rosie could never have had guts to persue. There was also rats scouring through, and crickets, but they got to the end opening, which turned out to be the Abbey ruins. "Here we are again, why doesn't this surprise me?" said madame Zhoux. "I had an incline that it would lead us hear," she said as they surfaced into the open air of the Abbey ruins. They walked around the ruins, the ruins ran roughly two hundred and fifty feet by five hundred feet in square size. They scoured through, looking for anything linking the ruins with the cult. There was fresh foot prints, and when they got to the centre where the alter once lay, there was drawings on the flooring of a massive haxagram, it was marked in blood. The blood was fresh, and it could have come from an animal, or even a human being. They scoured some more, and they came across old bones of animals, bits of feathers, and various artifacts, besides that there wasn't anything else. As they left the ruins, they came across Gilbert. He was walking his dog Milly, Milly was an old dog that walked with a limp, just like its master. It had three legs, and God knows what happened to the forth leg. She was a labrador, very fierce looking that it scared Rosie. The dog walked very slow that if she had decided to chase Rosie she would never catch up with her. She started barking fiercely at Rosie and madame Zhoux. "What are you doing here?" signed Gilbert, "do you know this is sacred ground," he signed. What are you doing here yourself, knowing that this is sacred ground?" responded Rosie. Gilbert didn't know how to react. "Has the cat caught your tongue," Rosie said with sarcasm. Gilbert simply ignored her, then carried on walking past. Him and his dog simply limped away. He walked a few yards, then turned back, and gave Rosie a scornful look, then he carried on walking. "What was that about? and what was he doing here? You don't think he knew that we was here?" madame Zhoux asked. "I think, he has been spying on us," suggested Rosie. They carried on walking, and they got back to Bramwell in no time. Madame Zhoux didn't stay long, she stayed long enough to have a cup of tea just to warm herself up, then she left.

Everytime, Rosie wanted to visit Rebecca, she was greeted with an excuse, it was either Rebecca was out, or she was ill. This time Rosie wasn't taking no for an answer, it was coming up to her birthday, and she expected Rebecca to be there, Trevor couldn't excuse her neither. Rosie's birthday was coming up on the Saturday, she was just going to have a family celebration. Trevor gave an excuse, he said that he would be working, and his parents were going to be busy that Saturday. It was a perfect opportunity for Rosie to have Rebecca all to herself.

Rosie was full of spirit on her birthday she was forty nine. She woke up early to go to the butchers, and the fish mongers. She bought the best cut of beef, and a couple of trout fish. At the fish mongers, she bought some fresh prawns, sea scallops, clams, mackeral, and lobster. Her family loved sea food, and that Saturday was going to be the day of a sea food fiesta. Toby and Robert were going to barbecue the mackeral, alongside beef burgers. Besides her family, Rosie invited madame Zhoux, Doctor Edelbert, Suzanna, and Father Thomas. To begin with Father Thomas was sceptical, he didn't have much to do with the outside world, but after gentle persuasion from Rosie, he agreed to come. Rosie didn't invite anybody else, not even her neighbours, Justin and Aida. Rebecca had to be there to help her prepare all that food, so she had no excuse neither. They all turned up, and the party was in full swing, madame Zhoux brought her tarot cards, and was doing readings for whoever wanted to have a reading, without charging any money. Suzanna and Doctor Edelbert turned up, he requested a day off last minute and it was given to him. John wasn't working that Saturday any way, but he was out, first thing in the morning, and he was in the company of Roger, Justin, and Mayor Jenkins. He had volunteered to do some charity work for the community, alongside Roger, Justin, and Mayor Jenkins. They were doing some charity of some sort, and it wasn't long before it was finished, that is when he showed up. He didn't turn up alone, he brought along with him Roger and his family, Mayor Jenkins and his wife Sheila. Trevor was also going to spend the weekend with his family, mainly with his father Justin. "We need a father son bonding time," said Justin to Trevor. He decided to go on a fishing weekend trip with Trevor. "You are of age now, and you can't live in sin, therefore you should make a wedding proposal, as soon as possible, before the village starts talking," persuaded Justin. Trevor was a bit perplexed by his dad's proposal, but he went along with it anyway. "This is a perfect moment for us to bond, and we should make the most of it," manipulated Justin. They went fly fishing in the mountainous rivers, and they camped in the outdoors.

Back at the party, Rosie was perplexed to see Roger, and Mayor Jenkins turn up, she had specifically told John, that it was only going to be a family celebration, but he had invited them anyway. 'He has done it again,' she thought. Now Rosie hated John, he was constantly bringing the enemy into the family, he couldn't be trusted anymore. She put up a brave face, and throughout the party she kept soliciting with Edelbert, Suzanna, and madame Zhoux, they gave her reassuarance. "He has gone too far this time," she thought. Father Thomas was the last one to arrive, he turned up because of politeness, he arrived one hour before the party finished, it was just merely to show his face, and save face at the same time. Rosie kept avoiding engaging into conversation with Roger and his wife, as well as Mayor Jenkins and his wife. John went out of his way anyway to keep them entertained, they were his main focus. Rebecca was in good spirit, she had helped Rosie with most of the food preparations, and she was also delighted to be spending time with her brothers, and mother. She also got to meet Doctor Edelbert, who had treated her in hospital, as well as meeting Suzanna, and madame Zhoux. Madame Zhoux was very much looking forward to meeting her, if she had had a chance, she would have loved to do a tarot reading on her, and much much more, so she could figure out what was really happening to her, from a spiritualist's point of view, but she never got the chance. The party was happening in the garden, there was over a dozen seats in the back garden, a gazebo, and a barbecue going which made Father Thomas comfortable. Rosie invited him in the house, she wanted to see if he had anything to say at all about his childhood experiences living at Bramwell. He refused to enter the house. "I would rather stay out here, thank you," he said politely. "Why don't you want to come in Father?" asked Rosie. Father Thomas looked around as if nervous, then replied, "Your house scares me, Mrs Lawrence. It has got so much horrible history, and so many tragedies and shall continue to," he replied. "Infact I have got to go now, talking about it, is bringing back horrible memories," he continued. He finished eating his barbecued mackeral accompanied by fresh salad, and potato salad, then he washed it down with a glass of white wine, then he said his good byes. As he walked away from Bramwell, he just shook his head, 'Lord have mercy upon their souls,' he said to himself, then he got in his car and drove off. "He knows more than he is letting out," expressed madame Zhoux. Doctor Edelbert, and Suzanna wanted to interrogate him about Bramwell but they never got the opportunity, because he didn't stay that long. He only stayed for less than an hour, as a man who lived by the schedule, he had given himself exactly less than one hour to stay at the party, and then after that he would leave, and that is exactly what he did. Doctor Edelbert, and Suzanna were disappointed, but there was always going to be another time. Despite Father Thomas' swift departure, it turned out to be a good party. After the party madame Zhoux and the rest left, leaving just the Lawrence family. Rebecca was going to spend the rest of the weekend at Bramwell. Tobin and Robert cleared up the mess after the guests left, while Rosie was catching up with Rebecca. It was so good for Rosie seeing Rebecca well again and blossoming, awaiting an engagement. Rosie couldn't help but be supportive, just to see her daughter happy. If she had her way, she would have forbbiden Rebecca solicitating with the Menderaz's, she wanted that relationship ending. She knew that they were part of the cult, and that they had a hidden agenda. 'Rebecca could do so much better,' she thought; but John would have none of it. "Trevor's father wants to push the engagement forward to a couple of weeks, you will be ready, won't you mother?" said Rebecca in an excited voice. Rosie was playing with Rebecca's hair, she had missed her so much. She gave her a tender kiss on the forehead, "Of cause I will be," she replied. "Justin wants to host the party, so it will be at his house, if you don't mind," she asked. "Whatever works for you dear, I will support you all the way," responded Rosie. Rosie was thinking of a plan to break their relationship, and have her daughter back home. 'The Menderaz's can't be trusted, they are a spawn of Carlos, and they mean harm to my family,' she thought. 'perhaps madame Zhoux can help stop the engagement,' she thought some more. On the exterior she appeared to be happy for Rebecca, but she harboured some deep concerns. After the party John disappeared again with Roger, and Mayor Jenkins. They caught up with Justin, and they went to meet up with other villagers. They met at the Abbey ruins, something was happening there, which wasn't known to John. They called it the ceremony of the harvest, it was to harvest all sacrificed souls, and to make them stronger and be linked more to the soul of Father Santos, in preparation for his return. John followed blindly, as long as he showed loyalty to Roger, Mayor Jenkins and Justin, everything was going to be okay. They gave John a black robe with a hood, "You are one of us now," said Roger as he handed him the robe. John wore the robe, and they led him to the alter while they were chanting away. Justin brought in a live goat, slit its throat at the alter, and Mayor Jenkins collected the blood in a chalice. After the chalice was full, Roger threw the goat in one corner, as if it had saved its purpose and was ready to be discarded. Mayor Jenkins passed the chalice to Roger, he started chanting in some weird language, then drank from the chalice. He passed the chalice to Justin. Justin drank from it, then he passed it to Mayor Jenkins, who did the same, and passed it all round the group. Lastly they passed the chalice to John who was still standing in the middle of the alter. John looked around, in puzzlement, he looked at Roger, then he drank from the chalice, and passed it back to Roger. They then danced around John and Roger, "You are one of us now," they shouted, as they danced. John felt a sense of relief, and he felt a sense of belongingness, that is all he had been yearning for, from the community. After the ceremony, Roger, and the villagers congratulated John, and it all ended on a good note for John. He got home late as usual, the rest of the family were still awake, and discussing Rebecca's upcoming engagement party, John couldn't have been happier. He spoke nothing of where he had been, but pretended he had been out at the public house with Roger. Rebecca was tired, she decided to go take a bath, before going to bed, the rest of the family was still in the drawing room, sat by the fire. She was in the bath for a while, and that is when they heard loud screaming coming from upstairs, it was Rebecca screaming. John and Rosie went flying up the stairs in hysteria, the bathroom door was locked. Rebecca screamed and screamed, and John tried forcing the door open but he couldn't. He ran to his garage, and came back with a sledge hammer. He managed to break the door down, when they got in, Rebecca was under water, she was drowning in the bath tub. They dragged her out of the bath tub, and she wasn't breathing. John resuscitated her, and a lot of water came out of her mouth, hence relieving her lungs. She started breathing again, and Rosie went to fetch dry clothes, some of her own, and brought a few blankets to warm her up. They took her to the drawing room, and sat her by the fire. Tobin, and Robert were in awe. Rosie went on to make her a hot drink, and before long she was fine again. "I don't know what happened, I was dragged under the water, and I couldn't fight," said Rebecca, her lips were still quivering. Eventually the mood calmed down, they chatted a bit, and they all decided to go to bed, it was early hours of the morning. "Rebecca, I think you should sleep in the spare room, it's all ready for you," said Rosie. "That's a good idea, after all these escapedes, that room is best for her," ejaculated Tobin. "Shut up Tobin, you know when to say all the wrong things," interjected Robert. "That's a fine idea," said John. Rosie took Rebecca to bed in the spare room," I will be at the other end of the floor, if you need me," she said, as she tucked Rebecca in bed. "Thank you mum," Rebecca said as she smiled away. Rosie shut her door, before going to bed herself. She left the boys downstairs with their father, they carried on chatting till before daybreak, and that is when they went to bed. Rosie couldn't sleep at all, she stayed awake while lying in bed. About five in the morning, the whole family was sound asleep, they were woken up again, by strange noises. It sounded like voices coming through the walls, they were chanting voices, and there was also banging on the walls. John couldn't be bothered to get out of bed, so Rosie got up instead, she went downstairs. The noises became very loud, she saw car flushing lights permuting through their curtains, and there was loud car beeping sounds coming from the front of their house. 'It must be Roger and his men beeping their car horns endlessly, and flushing their headlamps through their curtains,' thought Rosie. Rosie ignored the outside noises and distractions, instead she concentrated on the noises coming from within the cottage. The first person she checked on was Rebecca, she opened her bedroom door, the room was icy cold, and Rebecca lay there in silence. Rosie reached out and felt her cheek, she was icy cold. She shook Rebecca up in an attempt to wake her up, but she was out for the couch. She went and knocked on the boys bedrooms, but none of them responded, she was stranded in that room. It was getting colder and colder till icicles started forming on the edges of the furniture in that room. It became so cold that every minute passing, ice was forming so quickly, till she couldn't feel her toes and fingers. She shook Rebecca again, but she didn't awake. She couldn't physically drag her out of the bedroom, so she went and banged on the boys bedrooms endlessly until they woke up. Tobin and Robert eventually woke up, and they dragged Rebecca out of that bedroom. They dragged her downstairs to the drawing room, and they lit a fire, just to get her warmed up. In the mean time John was fast asleep. "What is this mum, it is like this house doesn't want Rebecca here," said Robert. After warming up a little, Rebecca woke up, she was still quivering, her lips had turned blue, and her finger nails purple. She looked up to her mother who was standing over her. "It's happening again mother, this cottage doesn't want me here. I don't want to be ill again, I must leave, and go back to Trevor, I feel safe with him," she said while quivering away, her whole body was shaking. She had planned on staying with the family till Monday, but now she changed her mind. "As soon as it's daybreak, I am going back home to Trevor. Everything was going so well, till I came here. I can't go mad again! I won't allow it." And surely at daybreak, she packed her belongings, and rung Trevor to pick her up. He turned up in no time, and she was back with him again.

Days that passed, Rebecca was beginning to forget about all the escapedes that happened to her at Bramwell. She was well again, and looking forward to her engagement party. Rosie felt more and more disturbed, but the boys were beginning to believe their mother, that there was an entity dwelling within Bramwell. They couldn't understand why it was only Rebecca's room that got iced up, while their bedrooms where nice and warm. As for the noises outside Bramwell, they couldn't care less about them. They were also shocked by their father's lack of response. "Do you believe me now?" Rosie questioned the boys. "We never doubted you at all, but you should learn not to be so sensitive," said Robert. "If you ignore it long enough it will go away, just get on with your life, like we are doing," suggested Tobin. "You suspect Justin, that much we know. Give us time, we will try dig some stuff from Trevor and Charles. Charles seems to be a nice enough guy, I will get it from him," reassured Tobin. Tobin was a flambouyant sociable guy, if anybody was to penetrate the Menderaz's family it will be him, he had charm and everything else.

Rebecca was back with Trevor, and life for her was running smoothly again. She became reluctant to get a job for herself, because Trevor was doing well for money working at the municipality. Rebecca told Trevor what had happened at Bramwell, and that she was never staying there again. He kept her safe, and became over protective of her, even from her own family, he loved her dearly. Madame Zhoux got more and more curious about what was happening at Bramwell, she started spending more and more time with her tarot cards, doing daily readings of Bramwell, she cared for Rosie and her family. Every reading she did, scared her more and more, and out of that she grew more and more concerned over the

Lawrence family. She remembered Rosie showing her an opening in the wall of Rebecca's old room. There was a safe which laid hidden behind the wall paper, and she couldn't find the key. 'The answer lies within that safe, and they had to find the key,' she thought. She called Rosie one afternoon, and started speaking of the safe. "Say nothing to John, about the safe, it is our only chance," she warned Rosie. Finding the key was going to be like searching for a niddle in a haystack, it was going to take a lot of time, patience and perseverance. Rosie didn't speak of it to any of her family members, she didn't even trust Tobin, and Robert, for all she knew, they could have been brainwashed as well by the cult. She never ruled out Father Thomas, his lack of enthusiasm didn't put her off trying getting help from him. He knew a lot, and he was a big part of the puzzle, that was going to bring an end to this cult. 'Suzanna might know something about the key, she did mention something about a key, after all,' thought Rosie. She had to meet up again with Suzanna, inorder to solve the mystery of the safe. Madame Zhoux recommended her meeting up with Doctor Edelbert, and Suzanna to find out more about the safe. Rosie rang up Suzanna, she was going to meet up with her at the library, without Edelbert, nor madame Zhoux, it had to be intimate. They met up on a Tuesday, Suzanna felt she was being watched and followed, and so did Rosie, that beige pick up truck was still following her about. The library was the most private place they could meet up. On that day Malachi was working at the library, he kept snooping on them, or pretended to be sorting out books close to where they were sitting, he was trying hard to eeves drop, so he could report back to Roger of what he had heard them talk about. Rosie and Suzanna were aware of his presence, so they tried to be as discreet as possible, they were whispering instead of talking out loud. He couldn't pick up a word of what they where talking about, his mission was unfruitful. "You mentioned a safe in Rebecca's old room. My sisters and I never discovered that, that is new to me," said Suzanna. "We found a key, but the key belonged to some box dad found inside the chimney wall. The key was inscribed SAC, and I don't know what my sister Charlotte did with that key, it could actually open the safe as well. "SAC, you said, I found the same inscription on a dagger that I found in my husband's sock drawers. I didn't speak of it, because I think he is working with the cult members. What does SAC mean?" asked Rosie. "Well, it means Sacrificial Agents Chosen, we learnt that from a priest, I think it was father Francis. You mean your husband has got a dagger with those inscriptions! be careful of him! he has been brain washed by the cult!" cried Suzanna. "Maybe that old key my sister and I found, is the same key, that can unlock the safe. Where that key is, I don't know, but it has to be somewhere in the cottage. I believe my sister hid it somewhere in the cottage," she expressed. "I can tell you a lot, even about the ritual we did, that ended up killing my family. We got help, from a Father Francis, but he too perished during the ritual. He gave us silver coins, for our own protection, that is the only reason why Doctor Edelbert and I survived the ritual," she proceeded. Rosie was just listening, and absorbing all the information as they whispered in the library. Malachi was always close by, trying so hard to listen to their conversation. "If you can try get hold of that dagger, because John might use it on you, I mean sacrifice you to the cult. Get hold of the dagger and destroy it, you can do so, by throwing it in fire, it is silver after all, and it will perish in fire," she insisted. "That dagger is part of their plan, destroy it, and you will slow them down," persisted Suzanna. "Mrs Lawrence,,, I lost my whole family, to this cult, believe you me, nothing is going to stop them from murdering your family, for their own cause. These are sick, twisted individuals, who think that they are going to be immortals, they will do anything, even if it means murdering your whole family, they will do that," she warned. Rosie had a dilemma, should she try convince her kids to leave the village with her, or stay and fight. It seemed like a losing battle, at the same time none of her kids were willing to leave the village anyway. She had tried that already, and failed. She felt cornered, but she had to fight for her family; she did have adequate support after all. "Going back to the key, my sister and I found it inside the air vent in Charlotte's room, which is Rebecca's former room. A swam of flies flew through that air vent, all supernatural you know, that is what led us to open the air vent and search inside there. Low and behold, there was a key with inscriptions SAC. Dad got curious and went searching everywhere in that room. From the fire place Charlotte had seen a ghost of some old woman, who kept pointing at the fire place. Dad dug his hand inside the chimney walls, that is when he felt a box, he got it out. And on the box was an inscription SAC. The box was locked, and we tried opening it with the key, and it worked. We opened the box and inside was the big black book. They call it the book of the dead. It later turned out that the book was a decoy from the real book, it was a replica, Carlos had been hiding the real book for years. The replica and the real book both had the inscriptions SAC on them. SAC is the secret in everything that they do, once my dad's car was spray painted by the villagers in the same inscriptions. Dad even had his car tyres spray painted SAC by one of the villagers. Their behaviours were mainly discrete, and other times they were right in front of your face. There is a Father Dowling though, who helped us indirectly, but he has since disappeared from the village," continued Suzanna, she sounded exhausted just trying to relive the horrible experiences. Malachi was still hanging around very close to them, he kept pretending to be sorting books out on the book shelves close to where they were sitting. After hearing all that Rosie didn't need to second guess herself, what she was perceiving as reality was actually happening, often she had felt in her mind, that her mind was so disturbed, equivalent to someone who was on hallucinogens. These villagers were intentionally harmful, and dangerous. Rosie had lost all faith in her family, little did she know that Robert and Tobin were having private discussions between themselves about what was going on at Bramwell. They believed their mother, and they were working on a plan, to penetrate Justin's home, and dig for information from Charles and Trevor. Trevor was too smitten with Rebecca, he had no idea of what was going on, but Charles was open minded. Even Rosie thought of penetrating Aida, after all, she could have been ignorant of the goings on with Justin. Aida was a timid woman anyway, always submissive to Justin, she was more like the slave of the family, catering for everybody's needs in the family, without questioning. That is what Justin expected of her, and she delivered without question. Justin was a domineering character, he controlled his whole family, and those around him. 'A woman's place, was to be submissive to her husband, and the children, submissive to their father, 'that was his motto, and that is how he had been brought up. Suzanna was to visit Rosie, and help her search for that lost key, it had to be somewhere inside Bramwell. They ended on a note, that Suzanna was going to help her all the way through. They left the library, and left Malachi feeling disappointed because he wasn't able to hear any of their conversation. The minute they left the library, Malachi rang Roger and told him that he had nothing for him. "Never mind," replied Roger, "we will get them another time," he ended the conversation. Suzanna went back to Edelbert's apartment, and Rosie went back to Bramwell.

Rebecca was feeling bored and more or less isolated at her new home with Trevor. While Trevor was working, he was working long hours, she sat home twiddling her thumbs through boredom. She decided to start looking for work, but up to no avail, she was wondering why she couldn't get a job in the village, even in a grocery shop. It was part of the cult's ploy conditioning her to think that she was unemployable. She started missing her family, and so she invited her mother over for dinner. She told Trevor about it, and in turn Trevor invited his mother and father as well for the dinner. Rebecca had planned on making a heart warming meal, as it was winter, she chose braised deer, boiled new potaoes, with a mixture of vegetables, but mainly carrots, followed by an apple pie with custard. Rosie turned up early to help her with the preparations. She turned up around lunch time, and they both went to the shops to buy the ingredients. They also bought some fresh herbs, and apples for the pie. "Mum's recipe is always the best," she said gleeing away at her mother, as they shopped for the fresh herbs and apples. "That's is right," smiled Rosie. Lastly they went to George's for some deer meat, he had variety of all game, which forced Rebecca to buy some pheasant as well. "What is the occassion? dare I ask," George was enquisitive. "Just a family dinner," replied Rebecca. "I hear Justin and Aida, are going to be joining you for dinner. Give my love to him will you, jeered George. His smile was sarcastic, that Rosie and Rebecca picked up on it. "I only look out for my own," he jeered some more. Rosie and Rebecca were speechless, they left the butchery. From the butchers they decided to eat out for lunch, so they went to a small cafe, called Tiffanny's. It was owned by an old lady called Tiffany, she had been in the business for years, and was well known for her excellent pies. She made both savoury and sweet pies. Her favourite sweet pie was pumpkin pie, because pumpkins were always in season in the village. Tiffanny was a sweet old lady, in her seventeenties, she worked alone in the cafe, and had done so most of her life. Strangely enough, she used to be a very close friend of Audrey's, every now and again they used to meet up at the local charities. They used to work together in soup kitchens, and such like, to raise money for various charities in the village. "I hear Audrey's son is now living next door to you?" she asked Rosie. Tiffany was an extremely cheerful old woman. "That must be something for you, I used to hear all sorts of strange stories about Audrey and Carlos, but I am a woman who minds her own business. We were friends, but we never went to each other's houses, if you know what I mean. I keep myself to myself," exclaimed Tiffany. "Mmmm," that was Rosie's only response, she wanted her to talk some more. Since Rosie and Rebecca sat at the first table next to the kitchen, Tiffany kept talking to them while she served their food. "I was born in this village you know, just by the creek. Overtime, I have seen so many people come and go from that cottage of yours. Most of it we were not allowed to talk about, even as kids. How are things going for you there? By the way I am Tiffany, everybody in this village knows me," she said. She reached her hand out to shake hands with Rosie and Rebecca. Rosie and Rebecca shook hands with her, and introduced themselves like wise. Rosie and Rebecca had gone for the cornish pasties, macaronni cheese and salad. Tiffany finished serving them, she brought their lunch to their table, then she sat herself down with them. Since Rosie and Rebecca were the only customers at that time, Tiffany sat herself down with them and carried on chatting. "It's not often that the shop is this queit, so I have to sit down while I can," she expressed, she did enjoy a good nutter, and there wouldn't have been better timing. In appearance Tiffany looked very much like Audrey, short, grey haired, and struggled walking. One could have easily mistaken them for sisters, but they were not related. "I grew up in the village, and I have got fond memories of my childhood, my father never used to allow me and my brothers to go anywhere near Bramwell. He used to say, strange things were happening there, and he didn't want us there. Tiffany coughed a bit then proceeded, "I had two brothers who have since passed, Jerome, and Jediah, they were both younger than me, but I managed to outlive them. My father was once Mayor to this village, he was a respectable man, who had to deal with a lot from some of the villagers," she took a sigh, swallowed hard then continued. "He believed that there was some witchcraft, or occulting happening in this village. They killed him you know, and he was only fifty two. He was found impaled at the Abbey ruins. Noone ever caught the culprits," she whispered. Her eyes where dilating with excitement, because finally she had found some people who had the patience to listen to her nutter away continuously. "They believe it was the cult members who worship their leader, who once lived in your cottage," she said in an excited manner. We never talk about it, because rumours have it that if you talk about the cult, they will sacrifice you to their serpent god. My mother said that noone was willing to investigate the death of my father. He left us enough money, that my mother and I were able to start this cafe, and it has been in the family ever since. Tiffany had two boys of her own, but as soon as they came of age, they left the village for the city, and had never returned, not even to visit her. My husband Jack died many years ago of tuberculosis, and I have always forbidden my two boys from ever visiting me here," she continued. She leaned forward to whisper in Rosie's ear, "Some people believe this village is cursed, that is why I forbid my boys from ever coming here. I haven't seen them in over thirty years," she whispered. She sat back in her chair then said, "What do you think of the village?" she asked Rosie. Rosie could clearly see that Tiffany was a gossiper, but nevertheless, Tiffany told her some very important information about the village. "Rumours round the village has it that, there is a demon dwelling in your cottage. Well, that's what people are saying," added Tiffany in an excitable manner. "Many people have died in that cottage of yours you know, you could be next, for all we know," she agitated. "I don't mix with the rest of them you know, so if you ever need to talk, come talk to me," she urged.

Rosie and Rebecca finished eating their lunch, and left Tiffany's to go start preparing for Rebecca's dinner party. On their way back to Rebecca's they bumped into Isabella, she had just finished work at Almer primary school, she was on route to Tiffany's. "How pleasant to meet you," she said, I hear you have got a dinner party with Justin and Aida. Bless Aida, she is such a timid woman, and don't know what she is getting herself into. Poor Justin he had always been so promising for the village, and he ended up with a woman like her. He could have done so much better for himself. Anyway we will soon find out," said Isabella. "Where are you coming from, that we haven't all heard about," she questioned Rosie. "Everybody round here knows at all times what everybody else is doing and going," she added. "We're coming from Tiffany's, we went there for lunch," responded Rosie. "Oh! now friends with Tiffany hey! everybody round here knows her to be a gossiper," said Isabella. "I heard that you are also friends with Thomas, he calls himself a priest, but he ain't no priest. You really have it for these village outcasts. Still, isn't it a shame about old Ms Biggs, and one armed Joe, they shall be greatly missed," she said in a zealous manner. "Do you know, old Tiffany, Ms Biggs, and Audrey Justin's mother, were all friends. They were a bit different to the rest of us. They brought trouble to themselves," added Isabella in a calous manner, "You don't want to be next, do you?" she jeered, then left. She went straight to Tiffanny's for some pie. Old Tiffany was scared of Isabella, Isabella was well known for tattle telling to the cult members. She was the one who tattle telled on Ms Biggs, that is why Ms Biggs ended up being put on a torcher stake by the cult members. It was also her who tattle telled on one armed Joe, she had been spying on him, when she spotted Rosie coming out of his cottage. She went to report the pair of them to Roger, and Mayor Jenkins. Nothing really registered with Rebecca, she was too smitten with her love for Trevor, all she thought about, was how to impress his parents when they turn up for dinner, and she was counting on her mother to make that happen. All she spoke about was Trevor and how well he was looking after her, and Rosie didn't want to spoil that, nor take that bit of happiness away from her. When they got back to her cottage, they got busy clening up, and making sure that everything was perfect. Some of the furniture in the cottage belonged to late Ms Biggs, including the bed that her and Trevor were sleeping on. 'How eeiry it seems, sleeping in some dead woman's bed,' thought Rosie, but Justin had reassured the young couple that he had bought the furniture off. 'From who,' thought Rosie, 'old Ms Biggs had no living relatives, it was Roger who took her house after she died, and pretended that he had bought it,' thought Rosie. She knew the truth, from what one armed Joe had told her, he had connotated to her that old Ms Biggs left her cottage to him so he could sell it, and move away from the village. Since he was dead, nobody will ever know the truth. Perhaps his brother Father Thomas could vow for him, but since they were estranged, there was no chance of that ever happening. 'Did Isabella connotate that the cult was going to get rid of Aida, and replace her with one of the villagers, who better to be the one, than Isabella herself. Isabella was a spinister who had always been unlucky with men, she had dated a few men in the past, but none of them wanted to commit to her. They always ended up marrying other women. She joined the cult, and in return had promised her a husband, but she had to be patient,' Rosie thought. At some point in her youth, Isabella had been in turbulent relationships, whereby she ended up having backstreet abortions which resulted in her becoming barren. She had indulged in various affairs with including, Roger, Mayor Jenkins, and many others, and now she was waiting for the cult to get rid of poor Aida, so she can be the next Mrs Menderaz, she was counting on it. No doubt Isabella was going to George's after being at Tiffany's, she was dying for some juicy gossip, and George always told. George the butcher had been in the cult for about most of his life. His life didn't start that easy, he was brought up in a family of two, him and his younger brother, brought up by alcoholic parents. Him and his brother Steven grew up with such neglect from the parents, that the cult members stepped in, and took care of them. It was Roger's parents who took them in, and groomed them into the cult. The minute Steven came of age, about ninenteen years old, he ran away to the city. Noone in the village ever heard from him again. George stayed, and he grew up with Roger, and it was Roger who later helped him set up his business as a butcher. From the minute

Roger's parents took him in, George took an oath that he would be loyal to that family for as long as he lived. George was married to Gladys, a local woman, and they had four kids together, three girls, and one boy. His wife was well known in the village, and very much disliked. She was known to be a trouble maker, a gossiper, and a home wrecker. She had multiple affairs, and was constantly interfering with other people's children. She was always calling other parents, bad parents. Often she would get the cult involved, which resulted in families seperating, and all the time she appeared to be the heroine, the cult admired. They were even consulting her, on what should happen to those poor kids. A lot of them ended up being under the care of the cult members, and she would be rewarded in money. At some point the police had gotten involved with her own children, the children had complained to their school that they were being abused at home by her. It became a big police matter, that the police took her kids away from her, and put them in care. She was lucky that Mayor Jenkins stepped in, and they were given back to her. She claimed to be a religious woman, who never missed Sunday service, but her true heart was very sinister. It was funny that her and George fostered kids, there was streamless number of kids, who were passed on to her and her husband by the cult. They in turn would groom these unfortunate kids into the cult. Some of them ended up being sacrificed, and the remaining became cult members. Some were used as sex slaves by the powerful men of the cult, like Mayor Jenkins and Roger. Gladys had close relatives in the village, a lot of them were cult members, the few who were not, had misconstrued ideas about her as a person. They said she was a deacon in the church, or a prayer warrior. Little did they know that she was a devil worshipper. Rachel, one of her sisters suspected her of foul play, she had spent a lot of time with her and her family in the past, and had witnessed a lot of things that brought her into suspicion. Rachel had spend one summer with her family, while George had been taken ill in hospital with heart problems. He was confined in hospital for three months, and Gladys had asked for Rachel's help. While Rachel had been there with the family, she saw so many cult members come and go, and all the time she was eves dropping. That is how she knew that Gladys and George were part of some satanic cult. She heard Gladys talk with some of these people about sacrifices, and ceremonies. When George got better and was discharged from hospital, Rachel left, and never returned. Since Gladys and George had been comfortable, both financially, and in the cult, Gladys had been made responsible for one of the cults members twins. They were falling out of line, and Gladys was the chosen one to take those children in, and was rewarded handsomely.

Chapter 9

Rosie and Rebecca got back in plenty of time to start preparations for the dinner party, firstly they cleaned the whole cottage, and Rosie laid the new table cloth that they bought in the village centre, then laid some candles. They went on to prepare the pheasant, by stuffing it with sage, and some other herbs, then basted the deer in herbs as well. They even had time to have a cup of tea and a chart. Since Rosie couldn't have that quiet word while they were in the village centre, now was the time. "Are you happy Rebecca, does Trevor make you happy?" she enquired while they sat by the kitchen table. Rebecca started twiddling her thumbs, "Yeh, I guess so. He takes good care of me," she replied. She couldn't look in her mother's eyes. "He makes me feel safe, and he does things for me," she added. Rosie took a gallop of her tea, then swallowed hard, she seemed concerned by her reply. "Do you love him?" she asked. "I guess I do! well I think I do!" she replied abruptly. "What has this got to do with anything?" she asked in a defensive manner. "It's only that, I care about you, and I do not want you to make a mistake," responded Rosie. "His parents treat me well, and they make me feel welcome in their family," she interjected. "But Rebecca! that is not enough! Do you trust them! because I don't! I worry about your well being!" cried Rosie. "I am always here for you, remember that. Let's us not spoil the evening, and let's put up a good dinner party," Rosie reassuared. They soon went back to their cooking, Rebecca was in charge of the apple pie, while Rosie cooked the main meal. The deer was already braising in the oven, and so was the potatoes and vegetables. Everything was cooked in the oven, including the pheasant. Just before the food was ready for serving, Aida and Justin showed up, and they were followed by John. A minute into tucking in their food, Roger turned up, accomapnied by Mayor Jenkins. "We heard of the dinner party, and we were not going to allow that to pass us by," said Mayor Jenkins. "We have got to thank John and Justin, for inviting us here," said Roger. "I hope you don't mind!" they both said at the same time. Rebecca was only there to please her in laws, and Rosie chose to go along with the flow, but deep down she was suspicious of the lot of them. She went out of her way, and went as far as even carving the meat, and dishing out everything else for everyone. She tried hard to stay in conversation, without showing signs of distress. Even John was proud of her. He got up and proposed a toast to his dear wife, for helping make such a beautiful evening. "We were thinking of pushing the engagement to next weekend," blurted Justin. "These two make such a lovely couple, I thought why wait hey!" he cheered. They all lifted their wine glasses to Rebecca and Trevor. "Roger and I are here to make things happen," Mayor Jenkins cheered.. "Next weekend it is!" cheered Roger. After the main course they had the apple pie, which was divine, and they all thanked Rebecca for putting up such a wonderful spread. After the dessert, Roger, Justin, and Mayor Jenkins disappeared to sit by the verandah while they indulged on their Brandy mainly talking about how promising Isabella was becoming in the cult. "She could be the next Mrs Mendereraz!" jeered Roger. They all laughed at Aida. The ladies and Trevor cleared up, and washed the dishes. The evening was a success as long as Rebecca and Trevor were concerned, and everybody went back home satisfied, except for Rosie. She was the last to leave, John had left with Roger and Mayor Jenkins, only God knows where they went to. She bade her daughter goodbye, and they arranged to meet again in a couple of days. Rosie wanted to make sure that her daughter didn't feel isolated from her family. If anything the cult was good at, it was isolating its victims, and Rosie was very much aware of that. She too was playing a game. She went back to Bramwell with her head geered onto solving the problem that was happening to her family.

Something dawned on Rosie, even in the dust of confusion; it was the key, and the safe she found hidden within the wall of Rebecca's room. 'The key! the key!' she kept saying to herself. Suzanna had mentioned something about a key, and it had to be somewhere in Bramwell. She met up with Suzanna, except this time she invited her to Bramwell. It was an early Tuesday afternoon that Suzanna showed up, Doctor Edelbert was working, and so was John, the twins were in college, what better opportunty to scour through Bramwell for the key. They started the day with a cup of coffee, then to talking. "There is secret places in this cottage," started Suzanna. "I lived here, you know. We shall start downstairs," she declared. They started in the kitchen, till no table was left unturned, but they couldn't find the key. Then they moved into the drawing room, and the lounge, but still couldn't find the key. They then moved to the bathroom upstairs, by then Rosie knew of the opening in the bathroom flooring opening up to a passageway leading to the Abbey ruins. Besides that there was nothing else hidden, they moved on to the boys bedrooms, scoured through everything, but they couldn't find it. From there they moved to the spare room; then Rosie and John's bedroom, but they couldn't find anything. They had gone with a fine toothed comb, but still without a result. Lastly they went into Rebecca's bedroom, Rosie knew that there was something there, that is why she left it till last. From last experiences Suzanna knew that a lot of clues to the phenomena lay within that room. Lastly they searched in Rebecca's room; the mood in that room was dolorous, one couldn't help but feel the depressive state of the room. Whether it was dolorous, depressive, or opressive feel of the room, it didn't matter, it had to be extrodited from that room. "The passageway in the flooring means something," Suzanna ejaculated. "But the passage way leads to the Abbey ruins," responded Rosie. "We all know that by now, there must be something else," she continued. "The fire place," exclaimed Suzanna. Suzanna got to the fireplace, she dug her hand inside the fire place, but she couldn't feel anything other than the brick. She got the torch and shone it through the chimney, all the way to the breast. Then she spotted a lose brick, she pulled it out, and then beneath the brick, she found the key. She pulled it out, it was a black key with inscriptions SAC. "Bingo! we found it!" she cried. "The key must belong somewhere," she said. It must be the key that opens the safe that I found in the wall. Here! give it to me, and I will show you," exclaimed Rosie. Suzanna handed the key over to Rosie. "Thanks!" responded Rosie. Rosie had never felt this confident in her whole entire life. She grabbed the key off Suzanna, and went straight to the wall that the safe was insitue. She placed the key in, and low and behold it fitted like a glove. It was the key needed to open the safe. She opened the safe, and inside the safe was an old book, more like a writing pad. It was a diary, with a white cover, inscripted SAC. The first page of the diary, read Father Santos. Rosie and Suzanna started reading the diary, it was written by Father Santos many years ago, and now they had it in their hands. Inside the diary was talking about the serpent cult, ressurection of the dead, and the return of the cult leader. They read stuff about hexagrams, sacrifices, and about the Abbey ruins. The Abbey ruins were sacred grounds for the cult, and had to be protected from being defiled by none members. Part of the writing in the diary was in plain English, and the rest was in a strange language as if coded. Neither Rosie nor Suzanna knew what language it was, never mind what it meant. In english, it read everything they knew already about the cult, but it was that strange language they couldn't understand. They needed an interpreter, perhaps Doctor Edelbert would know somebody who could interepret. Rosie and Suzanna had to protect that diary from the cult members. Rosie wasn't going to keep it in the house, especially with John prawling like a sniffer dog in that cottage, he would soon find it. They decided Suzanna should take it with her, and it would be between her and Doctor Edelbert to decide the safe keeping of the diary. Besides the fire place, they had done enough progress, and there was nowhere else left to look. Suzanna left Bramwell feeling enthusiastic, while Rosie was left feeling hopeful.

When Suzanna left Bramwell, she spotted a beige pick up truck parked just outside Bramwell. It had tinted windows that she couldn't see who was driving it. The pick up truck followed her all the way to Doctor Edelbert's apartment. The minute she drove into the flats driveway, the pick up truck drove past. Edelbert was working on shift at the hospital and he wasn't going to finish work until late that evening, Suzanna was patient enough to wait so she could give him an update of the daily events. She kept thinking about the beige pick up truck with tainted windows, and who was driving it. Back at Bramwell Rosie was pacing up and down, she thought of paying Aida a visit, so she turned up at her door step. Aida was in, and Rosie felt that maybe Aida might share something with her. Aida invited her in, and all she spoke about was Justin, how he was such a stubborn and difficult man. "I can never get to him about anything, and I have lived with him for over twenty five years," she said. "You are lucky to have John, he seemes to be a very conscientious husband," she added. Rosie didn't know what to say, except acknowledge that she was in a similar situation with John. Now the two women had something in common. "I have often thought of leaving him," declared Aida, "But it is the children that I stay for, they are old enough now to be brain washed by him," she whimpered. "I feel the same about John, if it is any consolation," Rosie stated. Rosie felt she could have an ally with Aida, and maybe join forces to get their husbands out of the cult. At the same time, she kept her cards close to her chest, she never mentioned anything about the cult to Aida, lest she was one of them, but one thing she knew was that Aida was an unhappy woman. They spoke mainly about mundane stuff, and every now and again she spoke about Justin's compulsive nature. It was a fruitless visit, one might say. Tobin and Robert was her closest allies, they were beginning to suspect that their father was part of some cult, and they definitely knew that the Menderaz family were part of something that didn't make sense to them. Tobin and Robert started spending more and more time with Trevor and Charles, they met up three times in every week, most of the time at Justin's. One day Rosie confronted her boys while John was out with Roger, Mayor Jenkins, and Justin. She had the boys all to herself for most part of the evening. "I want to talk to you boys," she began. She got the boys in the drawing room, made some tea, and they were sat in the drawing room. "I am sure you are not blind, and that you have been noticing some strange things happening here. I feel your father is part of some cult here in the village. Roger, Justin, and Mayor Jenkins are part of it, and I am sure you have heard rumours about our cottage being part of it as well," she spoke with an authoritative voice. You are old enough to know," she exerted. She wasn't going to tell all, because she didn't know to what extend the boys had been brainwashed by their father, and the village. Robert and Tobin just sat there on the comfortable settee next to the fire place, they looked bewildered. They kept staring at the floor, afraid to give eye contact to their mother. It was Robert who spoke first, "Mother, we believe you, we have spoken about it, between ourselves, and sometimes to Charles and Trevor. We know, so don't worry," said Robert. "We know mother," repeated Tobin, "we are not blind. If there is anything you want us to do," reassured Tobin. Rosie reached out to her boys, then held their hands, in a comforting manner. "I want you to find access into Justin's office, I tried myself when I went there with madame Zhoux, we sneaked into the house, but the office door was locked. Find a way to get those keys, and find what you can from there," Rosie said. "There is something hidden there," she insisted. "I will see to that mum," replied Tobin. "Everytime we spend at Charles' place, Aida and Justin are always out, and that will be perfect opportunity to get into the study room, they always leave the house keys behind," continued Tobin. Rosie felt better knowing that she was getting support from her boys. "These days Trevor hardly spends time there anyway, so it will be easier for us to deal with just Charles. One of us will distract him, while the other fishes around and finds access to the office. I would like to be the one who opens that office door," declared Tobin.

Chapter 10

Days that followed, Rosie felt watched and followed about by different people, she kept bumping into old Jimmy, and Isabella. Old Jimmy was everywhere she went, from the library to the shops, butchers, and the market. At the same time Doctor Edelbert was being stalked by Mayor Jenkins' henchmen, and also by Roger. He had to be careful in his descretion, that he had to minimise his movements. When Suzanna got the diary, she shared it with Doctor Edelbert, they were busy in his apartment reading the diary. As part of the diary was written in a strange language, they had to find an interpreter, what other place could they find one, than the library. In the library worked a linguistic man, and interpreter named Albert Foysther, he had done lot of work on ancient languages. Suzanna and Edelbert went on to meet him, they took the diary with them. While they were in the library, they spotted Roger, and Isabella in the library. Isabella and Roger were pretending to look for books close to where Suzanna, and Edelbert were sitting, Malachi stood right at the other end of the library. Roger and Isabella were the spies who would give feedback to Mayor Jenkins on what Suzanna and Edelbert were talking about. Albert Foysther was an educated man, with vast travel experiences, he was a man of intergrity, they felt they could trust him. They sat in one corner of the library, and they communicated by whispering to each other, or written notes that they passed on to each other. He was able to interpret the language in the diary, it was an ancient mesopotamian language. From the library, Suzanna and Edelbert went to visit Father Thomas, they took the diary with them hoping that he knew of its existence. They got to the vicarage, and the house keeper answered the door, an old lady in her sixties, with long grey hair, and of modest appearance. "Can I help you?" she asked. She was less than five foot tall, more like a midget. "If you want Father Thomas, he can't see you, he is asleep," she said abruptly. She was about to shut the door in their faces, that is when Edelbert blocked the door from shutting using his foot. "It is very important, and we have got to see him promptly!" he exclaimed. Dorothy was her name, she let them in. "Wait here I will get him for you," she said. Father Thomas was praying inside a little shrine that was within the vicarage. It was a small room no more than seven foot by seven foot. He had spend most of the day praying and was also fasting. He was on a forty day and night fasting. "He is fasting!" and don't appreciate being disturbed," Dorothy blurted. Suzanna and Edelbert knew what he was fasting for. "It is okay, we still want to see him," insisted Edelbert. Dorothy went to speak to him, and he came out like a shot. The guilty conscience was eating him up, he had to see them. He led them to the lounge and dismissed Dorothy. "You are dismissed for the day, I need some time alone," he said to her. Dorothy was out in a matter of seconds. "Your dinner is all prepared for you sir, all you need to do is put it in the oven," she said before grabbing her umbrella and hand bag, and leaving. It was perfect for Suzanna and Edelbert. Father Thomas smoked a pipe, like many priests in the church, he also drank brandy. "Do you care for some brandy?" he asked Edelbert. "Yes, neat I take it," responded Edelbert. "What about you Suzanna? do you care for some coffee?" Suzanna agreed to the coffee because they were going to be there for a while. He poured some brandy for Edelbert, gave it to him, then went to the kitchen to make some coffee for Suzanna. She took it black, with no sugar. They sat in the lounge, then he began, "What can I do for you. I heard about you from Rosie from Bramwell. "What do you want from me?" he asked as he smoked his pipe and sipping from his brandy. "We want you to help us," said Suzanna. "Help you do what?" he asked. He was playing with the hairs at the back of his head, he was bold anyway in the middle of his head. "Help us get rid of the entity dwelling in Bramwell," stated Suzanna. "It has killed so many people already, including my family," insisted Suzanna. "Listen my child, you can't tell me anything that I don't know already. Father Francis was my friend, learning that he perished over Bramwell, it hurts me," said Father Thomas. "Father Dowling is also my friend, I talk to him all the time. We mainly talk about the cult, and Bramwell. My brother died because of the cult, so I know what I am talking about," he declared. He cleared his throat then proceeded, "I know everything about the cult, I grew up with it, and I know all the members of the cult." Suzanna and Edelbert couldn't help but feel better. "Father Dowling is now living in a monestary about seventy miles out. He comes here regulary, to talk about the cult and Bramwell. I told him to lay off, but because of his stubborn nature, he can't do that," said father Thomas. Rosie told you that, because I learnt that she had been talking to my brother, the late one armed Joe. Talk to Rosie and she will tell you all about him. I lost touch with my brother since he betrayed our family to that cult, and they all died because of it. Since then I never forgave my brother, till his dying day. I didn't even go his funeral. So listen to me! you are not the only ones in pain, and as for Bramwell, I can't help you there," he disputed. "What do you want from me?" he questioned. "We want you to help us defeat the entity in Bramwell, and destroy the cult!" exclaimed Edelbert. "We can protect you! Safer by numbers hey!" Edelbert exclaimed. Father Thomas rubbed his head while pulling on the few grey hairs he had, he smoked on his pipe, then replied. "You are right. This is the reason I became a priest. I will talk to father Dowling. He doesn't want anybody in the village knowing about his whereabouts, but I will talk to him. I am sure if I mention Suzanna, he will be here like a shot," responded Father Thomas. "Do you know Roger stole from your brother. Ms Biggs' house was left for him, and Roger stole that under handedly, he knew Ms Biggs lawyer, and the lawyer never brought up the paper work after her death. He tells people he bought that cottage, but he didn't. Mayor Jenkins supported him with his freudulant activities," exclaimed Suzanna. "What a mind job!" cried Father Thomas. "I will get in touch with Father Dowling, and I will get him here in no time," he proceeded. Expect to hear from me in a few days," he added. Suzanna and Edelbert were not satisfied.

Suzanna insisted on Father Thomas giving them Father Dowling's address. After a great moments of thought, Father Thomas gave the address. "Thank you," said Edelbert as Father Thomas passed on the address to him. Suzanna and Edelbert were satisfied, they left the vicarage, and Father Thomas continued with his prayers.

Chapter 11

Father Dowling had taken refuge at 'The good sisters of mercy convent, he had been given immunity to stay there after he explained to the chaplaincy what he had experienced concerning Bramwell, and the serpent cult, and that the cult members were after him. He explained to the monsignor at the convent, and the monsignor a Father Samuel, had agreed to support him all the way. Father Samuel had heard rumours of Bramwell, and the extra ordinary happenings there. He grew interested in the subject, that he became very close to Father Dowling, so that he can dig some information from him concerning Bramwell.

Once having the address of Father Dowling, Suzanna and Edelbert decided to pay him a visit, they rung the convent first. He was delighted to hear from Suzanna, he had always thought of her, and had wondered how she was getting on. It was mother superior who answered the phone, she was quite abrupt to Suzanna, but she agreed to get Father Dowling on the phone. The phone at the convent hardly rang, unless if it was something of importance happening within the church, that is why she was surprised to hear a female voice over the phone. "Oh well, I will get him for you," that is all she said to Suzanna. Mother superior was called Margaret, sister Margaret as her fellow nuns addressed her. Mother superior was nearly eighty years old, and had been living in the convent for nearly sixty years. She hardly had any hairs left, the only few grey hairs she had, she hid under a coronet. All the sisters of mercy wore coronets that it was difficulty to differentiate one from the other. "Suzanna! how are you my child!" he cried. "I have often thought about you, and have kept you in my prayers. How is your friend Doctor Edelbert?" he cried. "What can I do for you, this time?" he asked. "It's happening again Father!" exclaimed Suzanna. "You mean Bramwell! I thought you left Bramwell!" he gasped. "No, I did leave, I mean there is a new family there, and Edelbert contacted me from auntie Doris'." she replied. "I see, what is it you want from me. What can I possibly do for you. I am done with that place, and I am not going back there," he responded. "Edelbert and I thought you could be of some assistance. We want to come up and see you," replied Suzanna. "Who told you of my whereabouts?" he asked, his voice sounded shaky. "Father Thomas did, you know, one armed Joe's brother. We know everything about him and Joe. He advised us to contact you, and that he will be happy to work with you to help the new family living in Bramwell," Suzanna expressed. "Your best bit of help was Father Francis; he knew everything, as for me, I was just a by stander, watching everything. I wasn't of any help to you, nor your family. I was a coward, and I still am, that is why I fled. Your best bit now is Father Thomas! I am sorry I can't help you!" he gasped. "Father Thomas send us to you, and he can't do it alone! he needs you. He is as frightened as you are! You are the priests, and Edelbert and I seem stronger than you two. Where is your faith Father!" Suzanna lost her temper. "You are priests, and you are meant to be strong in your faith, and protect that family," Suzanna insisted. After hearing Suzanna's plea, he agreed to meet up with Suzanna and Edelbert. "Promise that you wouldn't tell anybody of my where abouts!" he exclaimed. "Meet me here at the convent on Tuesday, that is the only time I am free, any other day I will be sunken in prayers, and tending to other duties," he agreed. "Tuesday sounds great," responded Suzanna. They agreed to meet, and the telephone conversation ended. Suzanna and Edelbert agreed on taking Rosie along with them to the convent, they thought if they brought her along, he would be more obliged to help, after he hears of her story.

 In the mean time Tobin and Robert were at the Menderaz's hanging out with Charles, Trevor was with Rebecca, and Aida and Justin were out having dinner with the Jenkins, Roger and John were there with them. It was a dinner party discussing the up coming engagement party of Rebecca and Trevor. The dinner party was being hosted at Mayor Jenkins house, it was full of the cult members. By that it meant that Gilbert, Malachi, George, and Isabel were there as well. Rosie didn't know anything of it, and she wasn't invited. Old Jimmy wasn't invited neither because he was a low ranking cult member, and was of no significance. Tobin and Robert knew what they had to do, Charles was alone in that cottage. They had planned it well that Robert will distract Charles while Tobin grabs the house keys and enter Justin's office. The plan worked, while Robert lured Charles to the back garden drinking, Tobin found the house keys on the kitchen table. He sneaked to the basement then got to the office door which was behind a book case, and there he tried different keys that was on the bunch, to see which would open the office door. It was the smallest of the keys, and it fitted, and he was able to get into the office. He searched in the office for any clues, he opened the desk, but he couldn't find anything, and he searched everywhere else to no avail. He looked everywhere else in the office, then he found a key hanging on the walls. It was a black key inscribed SAC. 'it must fit somewhere,' he thought. This time he went through the office with fine toothed comb. It was a small office anyway, no more than six feet by six feet. He scoured and scoured till he had to remove all the books that were lined up on shelves covering three walls of the room. He removed them all, then he found a safe hidden behind the books. The door of the safe was inscribed SAC. He tried to open the door using the black key, and to his surprise it opened the safe. He was astounded, inside the safe lay the big black book inscribed SAC. "I have found it!" he said excitedly. He got the book and placed it inside his racksack which he had used to bring beers for Charles, him and Robert. "I found it!" he said again. He put everything in order as he found it, then he locked the safe, placed the black key back into its place, then he locked the office door, and placed the house keys back onto the kitchen table before joining Robert and Charles in the back garden. He winked at Robert as a sign that he found something, Robert smiled. They hung around the Menderezas' for another hour then left, just when Aida and Justin were walking in.

    Back at Bramwell Rosie was waiting with anticipation, she had grown scared of being alone in that big cottage. The boys arrived and shared the good news with her. "We found it, the book!" shouted

Tobin. "It was there, in Justin's office as you predicted. It was tucked away in his office in the basement. I found two keys inscribed SAC, one was to open Justin's office door, and the other to open the safe. The book was in his safe," exclaimed Tobin. "We better look at the book, before your father comes back!" said Rosie in an anxious tone. They went to the drawing room, and Tobin pulled this big black book out of his rucksack. He placed the book on the table, and Rosie opened it. When she opened the book, there was a gush of wind that swept through the drawing room. "This book is important to them, and I am sure we are going to find out more about their secret," said Rosie. They flipped through the pages because they were short on time before John coming back. One page they read was about the formation of the cult, which was at the Abbey ruins, and that they practiced human sacrifices including sacrificing babies. It went on and on in description. The cult had been started over one hundred and fifty years prior. It spoke in detail about Father Santos who was the founder. He had taken the cult from his native land, and adapted it in the church because noone would ever suspect a church delging with satanism, and the occult. "Well done boys, I hope this book is going to set us free from this entity," Rosie cried. Rosie heard John's car pull up in the drive, she put the book back into the rucksack, and ordered Tobin to go and hide it in the storage room which was in the garden. Tobin did as suit, he buried the book beneath tonnes of storage containers. It was mainly piles of books that the family never used nor needed. "It will be safe there," urged Rosie. "Tomorrow I will dig it out and give it to Edelbert and Suzanna for safe keeping. When John came in, he was too tired to bother with anyone, he had had his dinner at Mayor Jenkins, he went straight to bed. Rosie and the boys sat by the fire till very late talking about the book; about John and how much he had changed; and about Mayor Jenkins and the rest of them. Rosie decided to tell all she knew to the boys about the cult." Don't trust anybody in this village because anyone could be one of them. Take for instance, your friends Charles and Trevor, Justin is a very active member of the cult. She told them about her meetings with Doctor Edelbert and Suzanna; she also told them about Ms Biggs tragic death, and about one armed Joe. She spoke of Father Thomas, and Suzanna's family who perished in Bramwell. She hadn't said anything before, because of fear of making them paranoid about the villagers. Now that she felt that their lives were in danger, she had to tell it all. Mostly she felt for Rebecca who being smitten by Trevor, made her most vulnerable. "How are we going to rescue her!" questioned Rosie, "It is going to be very difficult since the engagement is upcoming" she exclaimed. Of cause she hadn't forgotten about the silver dagger neither which was in John's sock drawers, she told the boys about it as well. "Who is he planning on killing?" asked Tobin. "He might be planning on murdering us all. You said the dagger is inscribed SAC, it was probably given to him by either Mayor Jenkins, or Roger, and even Justin for that matter. They seem to be the top of the chain of that cult. "Shall I get rid of it?" Rosie asked her boys. Tobin who seemed to be the smarter one of the two suggested she shouldn't meddle with it. "It is probably a trap to see how much we know of their cult. There again if you go on asking dad questions about it, he might alert the other cult members. "He is brainwashed by them, they did something to him, just like they have with Rebecca," added Robert. Robert wasn't really bought into the belief that the cult existed, it was all too overwhelming for him. As they spoke, he half looked bewildered by it all. "They seem to be watching us, and following us about, so be cautious boys," urged Rosie. "Be careful of where you go, and who you speak too, for they could be one of them. They have got eyes and ears everywhere," Rosie continued. "Roger seems to be too well off for this village, servants and all, how is he making his money?" questioned Tobin. "I told you about Ms Biggs, you tell me how he got her house. I am sure you have figured it out by now, how he became so wealthy. Mayor Jenkins lives extremely well as well, just like Roger, he has got servants and all," cuckled Rosie. "Why did we ever move here, it was all dad's idea, it was as if he planned this all along, now he is part of them. We should leave, and leave him behind with his precious Roger, Justin and Mayor Jenkins," Robert suggested hesitantly. "What about Rebecca? do you think I haven't thought of that," interrupted Rosie. "We have to stay and fight for your sister's sake!" she exclaimed. "Doctor Edelbert, Suzanna, and madame Zhoux, are helping us. Also there is Father

Thomas, Father Dowling, and a Father Samuel willing to help too. Rosie decided to leave the dagger where it was, and never spoke of it.

It was three days before the engagement party, it was to be hosted at the Menderez's. Rosie rang Doctor Edelbert at work to update him of her new findings. She had started a habit of ringing him even at work, and he was happy to talk. Doctor Edelbert always answered the calls without fail, that is how she knew that she could count on him. He was more or less at her back and call. "We found the book, it was at Justin's place!" she heaved over the phone. "The bastard had been hiding it all along," she said. "Shall I bring the book to you," she persued. Edelbert was busy with a patient, but he had to excuse himself to take the call. "Don't bring it to the hospital, I feel like I am being watched, even here," he exclaimed. "Meet me at my place about three o'clock, that is when I will be back home, Suzanna will be in as well. Then we can take it from there," he said. "I can't stay long on the phone, I have got patients to attend to. Speak to you later," he rang off, and went back to his patient. Edelbert had started thinking that some of the hospital staff were part of the cult, or at least were working for the mayor. Without fail Rosie turned up at Edelbert's apartment at three o'clock as arranged, she had the big black book in Tobin's racksack because it didn't fit in her handbag. Doctor Edelbert and Suzanna had been waiting in anticipation. "Welcome, I hear you found the book," exclaimed Suzanna as she opened the door to let Rosie in. "I'm not doing this just for me and my family, I am also doing it for you and your family. I still need a closure to what happened to my family," she expressed. Before Rosie got into the apartment, she was filled with great paranoia that she was being followed, she kept looking over her shoulders, and perpetually looking left and right to see whether there was somebody about, spying on her. She got into the apartment and they headed for the lounge. Rosie layed the racksack on the table, and then she got the book out, and placed it on the table. Suzanna and Edelbert opened the book, they started reading it out loud. It was a big book comprising of about two hundred and forty pages, it was going to take them a long time before finishing reading it. Rosie left the book with them, she had other fishes to fry, for instance finding a way to save Rebecca.

The Offering

It was early Saturday morning that the Menderaz's were preparing for Tobin and Rebecca's engagement party. They didn't contact Rosie, but John, he was over there like a shot. Justin and John spend most of the morning talking about, and planning the party. Isabella was in charge of the catering helped by George who supplied the meat from his butchery. Malachi was the one sorting out who was going to sit where; and Gilbert was in charge of the decorations, he was limping along all morning, acting all important. Poor Rosie had only to turn up that evening. She invited Doctor Edelbert and Suzanna, never mind the fact that they were not on the invitation list. They surely turned up together with Father Thomas, Rosie arrived a bit later, she was in a frenzy, Robert and Tobin got there before she did. She was fluffering about, shaking with worry about her daughter. Her hands couldn't stop shaking with fear. She got dressed in a red tunic dress, and a navy blue hat, and she wore black high heels, whereas Tobin and Robert were dressed casually. John got dressed at Justin's house, he took a three piece suit with him that morning. When Rosie arrived, he looked extremely smart in his grey suit, white shirt and a stripped tie. Justin had helped him with his hair, which was straight combed and jelled making a parting on the side. The Menderaz's family looked extremely smart as well, with the boys, and Justin, all dressed in texudo suits. Aida however looked a bit half hazard, she wore a yellow top and a green skirt, together with a red hat, the colours didn't match at all. Her hair was tied in a messy bun, and she wore a strange necklace which was a hexagram. There was many people at the party, nearly the whole village was there. Rosie noticed a strange thing about the guests, they were all wearing the same necklace as Aida, including the men. The women's necklaces were red in colour, while the men's was black. The only people without the hexagram necklaces was Aida and her boys, Doctor Edelbert and Rebecca, and Father Thomas. Father Thomas wore his church crucifix. The party had begun and was in full swing, Justin brought Rebecca and Trevor to the stage that he had created overnight. "We welcome! and congratulate this young couple, and hope that they will be good role models for the younger ones. We wish them a happy life together!" Justin toasted, as he stood by the pulpit. "Cheers everybody!" he joyed. There was tonnes of food, and alcohol, the men found themselves hanging around the bar area, while the women waited on the men. Rebecca and Trevor remained seated by the stage, and Rosie found time to have a word or two with her daughter. Father Thomas went up to congratulate them in person. There was so much activity that even him only managed to talk to the pair for a couple of minutes. Rosie went looking for Edelbert and Suzanna, she found them, they were busy chatting. As they spoke in the garden, Edelbert spotted a beige pickup truck with tinted windows parked in front of the driveway, it was in the road. He recognised the truck, and he told Suzanna about it. Suzanna was familiar to the truck as well. The truck was there for a good ten minutes before it drove away. Rosie was anxious, all she needed was to stop the engagement, and take her daughter away from the Menderaz's family. "Have You noticed something strange about these people?" she said to Edelbert and Suzanna. "They are all wearing hexagram necklaces, as if it's a symbol of something," she expressed. "What is the meaning of that, Father Thomas?" she perpetuated. Father Thomas was busy munching on his pidgeon and onion pie which Aida had prepared. "What did you say, pardon me I didn't hear you," he replied. He was lost in contemplation. "I said! they are all wearing hexagrams!" dictated Rosie. "I didn't notice, come to think about it, you are right," he responded. "Hexagrams is a sign that they belong to the cult. They only were them on special occassions to mark who they are. I learnt that many years ago," he continued. "We are really outcasts here," declared Edelbert. "That means that we ought to be very careful, mainly about what we talk about with them," he expressed. "I have noticed that Rebecca and Trevor are wearing the same necklaces, and John as well. What is the meaning of that Father?" questioned Rosie again in an anxiuos manner. Father Thomas took another bite of his pie. "These are really nice aren't they," he paused as he chewed along. He kind of looked lost in space as he was thinking, he held Rosie's hand. "It means that they are already initiated in the cult," he replied. "Doctor Edelbert and Suzanna showed me the book, and I had been conteplating on it. We need to find a way of destroying it. If we destroy the book, the cult is finished. The problem is that even if we were to burn it, it will keep reappearing. You tried that before, and it didn't work," he said that to Suzanna and Edelbert. There must be another way," he expressed. As they were talking Justin went to the pulpit to give a speech. In his speech, he kept referring to Rebecca and Trevor as special to the community. "These two are going to give us a new life," he kept repeating himself. Mayor Jenkins, and Roger went up as well, and kept calling them special. "This is what they do, and they have been like that for decades, bringing people up a pulpit, before killing them in a sacrifial ritual," said Father Thomas having been raised by Roger's family. As the party went in full swing Aida was just sat in a corner of the garden all by herself, that is when Rosie excused herself from Edelbert, Suzanna, and Father Thomas to talk to her. She was as quiet as a door mouse, she was grateful enough to talk to Rosie. Rosie saw that she was vulnerable, and vulnerable enough to spill the beans about the mystery of the necklesses. "I can get her to talk," Rosie said to Edelbert, Suzanna, and Father Thomas. "She seems like she is afraid of something," continued Rosie. She approached Aida, "Why are you sat here alone?" questioned Rosie. "It's your son's party, and you should be the soul of the party," said Rosie. "I know, I don't feel like I belong. I have always felt like I don't belong in this community," she grumbled. "Justin seems lost with his associates, I can't get through to him at all. I feel like I am the hat that he has to put on a hat stand. He spends most of his time with Roger, and Mayor Jenkins, and your husband of cause. I am nothing to him, and you are going to be the same with your husband. Sometimes I wonder why we moved here at all," she expressed. "There is something going on, and Justin keeps that away from me. Maybe you know! well! do you know!" she questioned, her eyes were wide open, she was bewildered. "Roger and Mayor Jenkins come along here every night, they disappear in his study. There they drink brandy till early hours of the morning. I would be way in bed when they leave. Your husband is always here as well," she gasped. "To begin with I thought he was having an affair, it wouldn't be the last, he has had several affairs in the past. Of late he has been spending considerable time with that Isabella woman. You know, the head mistress of the primary school. I hear she is a single woman. It is Roger, and Mayor Jenkins arranging their meeting ups. It was early months of our stay in the village, that I suspected. Now it is norm that they spend time together every evening, I mean with Roger, Jenkins and your husband," she gasped. "Do you suspect anything else, for instance the hexagram necklaces, you are wearing one as well?" questioned Rosie. "He gave me and the boys as a gift to make us feel part of the community. He told me everybody at the party will be wearing them, so me and the boys were obliged to wear as well," she responded. She was very sincere in her reply. "Do you know anything about Father Santos' cult? questioned Rosie. "Father who! I have never heard of him, all I know is I have lost my husband to his friends, and to that Isabella woman," replied Aida. "How come you are not wearing yours?" asked Aida. "Because we were not given any." Rosie responded. Aida was naive about the meaning of those hexagram necklaces. Rosie left Aida to rejoin Edelbert, Suzanna, and Father Thomas. "She doesn't know anything about the hexagram necklaces," she told them. "Mrs Lawrence, I would like to come to your house sometime this coming week, to bless your home," said Father Thomas. "I would like to help you. I can't stand the idea that your family might perish in that cottage just like mine did," he exclaimed. Rosie was pleased, she had haboured the doubt that Father Thomas could volunteer to help. "I appreciate that," she replied. "I don't want to turn up when your husband is there," he added. "Make sure he is out of the house, he works at the post office doesn't he?" he questioned. "Yes he does, and he is out during the day, and also in the evening he spends time with Roger, Mayor Jenkins and Justin." "They call it the club, where they spend most evenings," said Rosie. Aida kept trying to interact with Isabella, offering help with the catering, but every time she tried she got snubbed by her, so she left her alone. "Poor Aida," said Suzanna. "She looks so unhappy, her husband must be a bully or something," added Suzanna. It was Charles who went to rescue her, and spend the rest of the party by his mother's side. "Perhaps we should offer her a drink, she could do with a strong brandy," jeered Father Thomas. Rosie went and got her a brandy, she filled the glass up, she got her from Charles and she joined in conversation with Edelbert, Suzanna, and Father Thomas. Aida felt relieved, at least now she wasn't alone.

She drank her brandy very fast and before you know it, she became extrovert and out spoken. "You did need that drink," jeered Father Thomas. It was from that occassion that changed Aida, she started drinking a lot to musk her problems with Justin. She became an alcoholic in no time, that Justin couldn't handle her anymore that he send her packing back to her parents, and that is when Isabella became prominent in his family. Isabella started going there on a regular basis to help out with the cooking and cleaning. Everyday after work, she stopped by Justin's, that is when the rumours started going around that the two of them were having an affair. Before long she had moved in the Menderaz's home. Father Thomas felt bad, he felt responsible for the break up of their marriage.

After the party, Rosie and the boys went back to Bramwell, they found a dead bird on the front door, the head was missing, and on its body was the marking of a hexagram. "What is this! Is this meant to be a sign!" cried Rosie. She picked the dead bird and threw it in the rubbish bin that was by the front gate. "They are not going to stop, are they!" said Rosie to her boys. Inside Bramwell was icy cold, Tobin went on to light the fire in the drawing room inorder to warm themselves up. Robert went to fetch more fire wood from the back garden. The minute they started warming up, they heard a loud bang, the house was shaking, as if it were an earthquake. There was the sound of bells ringing in the house, from upstairs to downstairs as if summoning something. The sounds were deafening that they all covered their ears. The ringing of the bells lasted a good ten minutes, then the house shook again. Then there was the bangings on the walls, and they heard chantings coming from the walls. The markings on their bodies had way gone, but they reappeared again. It started with Robert, when he came in with the fire wood, as he lay the wood down next to the fireplace, his sleeves moved up, and that is when he recognised the markings on his arms. Rosie and Tobin checked their arms, and they had the same markings of hexagrams. "Mum just ignore it," shouted Tobin. Rosie couldn't ignore. "Can't you see this is a sign that we have been hexed, I mean marked for death!" she cried. The bangings carried on, that they could barely hear each other talk. "We are not running away!" declared Rosie. The fire then went out, and the cold escalated that they had to bring in some blankets from the bedrooms and covered themselves with them. They huggled in the drawing room, then the fire came back on again, and the cold in the cottage disappeared. Rosie went to the kitchen to fix some hot drinks, then she found a dead mouse placed on the kitchen table, it had strange markings on its abdomen. She picked it up and chucked it in the fire, which was now ablaze in the drawing room. While the boys were having their hot drinks, Rosie went to check upstairs to see if anybody was in there. When she got into Rebecca's room, there was a huge crack on one of the bedroom walls. It ran from the bottom to the top, the room was icy cold, that she could pick off bits of frost hanging onto the furniture including the bed. She went back downstairs and didn't say anything about it to the boys. John came in late, he had been with Mayor Jenkins, Justin, Roger and a few others including Isabella. Isabella was the only woman with high position in the cult, and a big influence, she was working towards becoming the priestess of the cult. John didn't bother to talk to his family, he went straight to bed ignoring all the commotions that was happening within Bramwell. He slept like a baby, while Rosie and the boys had a sleepless night, the noises were happening on and off till early hours of the morning. Rosie was the first one up while the boys lay in inorder to catch up with their sleep. She was up early to feed the chickens. She was in her night dress and dressing gown, she got the chicken feed from the garage, and went to the chicken coup. She opened the wooden cage to let the chickens out, but none of them got out. She went inside only to find all the chickens dead, they had been dicapitated, and the heads were nowhere to be seen. Their eggs had been smashed on to the wooden fence. Rosie cried and cried, she ran out of the coop, she didn't have anybody to talk to about it, the boys were fast asleep. She rang Father Thomas, who in turn had agreed to turn up that afternoon. He had agreed on blessing her house later on that following week, but he agreed to do it that afternoon. She also rung madame Zhoux, and she agreed to be there with Father Thomas when he blesses Bramwell. "I will bring my sage along, the prayers combined with my cleansing should rid Bramwell of the evil entity lying within," she said. Time moved so fast that before long it was afternoon, and Father Thomas arrived, but madame Zhoux was nowhere to be seen. Rosie and Father Thomas waited and waited, but she didn't show up. "Maybe something has happened to her," said Rosie nervously. "Anyhow we must proceed, we must start in the garden," said Father Thomas. He got his kit out of his bag. It comprised of the holy bible, an exorcist bible, a crucifix, and some holy water. They went to the front garden, Father Thomas was reading from the exorcism bible, he was holding his crucifix, and at the same time sprinkling holy water every part of the garden. They then went to the back garden, he was sprinkling the holy water everywhere while reading from the exorcism bible. Lastly it was the chicken coop, the dead chickens were still there, Rosie decided that it would be the boys' job to clear up after they have woken up. Father Thomas sprinkled the holy water in the coop, and from there they moved inside the cottage. They started off in the kitchen, he sprinkled the holy water while reading from the exorcism bible, then moved into the lounge, then the dining room, and then the drawing room before moving upstairs. By then the boys were awake, they came to greet Father Thomas, and were very compliant with what he was doing. He blessed their bedrooms, and spare room, and sprinkled the holy water in the rooms. Rosie didn't want to disturb John in the main bedroom, she was scared of how he was going to react towards Father Thomas. Little did she know that he had left early that morning after she woke up. He was at Rogers, he had heard Rosie and Father Thomas talking, and he had quickly gotten dressed and left Bramwell through the back gate. She opened the bedroom door quietly, and found out that he wasn't in. That is when she invited Father Thomas in the bedroom, he read from the exorcism bible and sprinkled the holy water. Lastly was Rebecca's room, Father Thomas saw the huge crack in her room. "What is this?" he asked. "Has this always been there?" he questioned. "No Father, this happened last night after the party. "Jesus Christ!" he exclaimed He sprinkled the holy water, and read from his exorcism bible. "This room scares me, I have got very bad memories of it. Your whole house frightens me Mrs Lawrence. He moved round the room, then he saw an air vent. He pointed at it. "That air vent has got something evil inside," he exclaimed. He moved towards the air vent, and sprinkled the holy water. Immediately a swam of bats flew out of the vent, they chased him out of the cottage. They were pecking on him on the face several times, till they disappeared into thin air. Rosie followed him to the front garden. He was petrified, but Rosie wasn't scared, because she had seen it all before. "Your house is evil Mrs Lawrence, it has always been evil, it has got the mark of the devil, even from my memories as a kid," he said. "Infact I don't want to go back in there, it is too dangerous," he said. "What are you going to do?" he asked in a concerned manner. "I don't know Father that is why I asked you here," replied Rosie. "Madame Zhoux was meant to be here with us, I hope she is alright!" cried Rosie. "Don't ever underestimate the powers of evil Mrs Lawrence," said Father Thomas. "I will talk to Father Dowling, and Father Samuel, perhaps the three of us can do an exorcism, no one priest can defeat this entity," he said. "I must go now, and you must remain strong in the faith of the Lord," he comforted. He was still holding his bag, crucifix and holy water. "Pardon me, I have to put these in the bag," he said while smiling away, he had regained his nerves. He opened his bag, and shoved in the crucifix and the bottle of holy water. "You shall hear from me soon," he declared as he opened his car door, then drove off. Rosie felt alone again, but with the boys awake she didn't need to be so lonely. "Your father apsconded again! it's typical of him. He should have been here to support us!" cried Rosie. "Don't be silly mum, you know he is never going to do that, supportive yah!" exclaimed Tobin. "Tobin is right mum, don't trust him because he is working with them," interceeded Robert. "From now on we don't tell him anything, we have got to keep our cards close to our chest, do you understand boys," exclaimed Rosie. It is hard for a woman not to trust her husband, but that is the way it had become for Rosie. "How come madame Zhoux didn't show up?" asked Tobin, they were sat in the drawing room where the fire was ablaze. She told the boys about the chickens being dicapited, they agreed to clean up. "It is like they sacrificed our chickens, or it was a sign of warning. Warning us that they are coming after us," said Rosie. John returned home, and Rosie tried talking to him about the happenings. He turned away, and told her that she was crazy, imagining all those things. He became isolated in the family, and felt like he had found a new family with Roger, Mayor Jenkins, and Justin. Every time he had conversation with Rosie or the boys, he was always praising the Menderaz's boys or Mayor Jekins family, as well as Roger's family. He wanted his family to be like them, compliant to the cult. "You need to see a shrienk," that is what he kept saying to Rosie. "You don't trust these people around here, and you don't even try to be their friend. There is something wrong with your brain," he kept saying to Rosie. Every time he spoke to Rosie, the boys would look at each other, none of them was brave enough to confront him. Tobin however managed to pluck up courage on that day, he confronted his father. "Can't you see you have been brainwashed by these people," said Tobin. John simply walked away, and disappeared into the lounge, he was smoking his pipe. He had become numb except when he was with Roger, Mayor Jenkins and Justin. The exterior he was trying to give off to his family was that, it was all shenanigans, more like mumbo jumbo nonsense. At least he was kidding himself to pretend to his family that the phenomenas were not real. Rosie was still concerned about madame Zhoux, she told the boys that she was going to check on her. By then she was washed and dressed, then she went to madame Zhoux'. When she got there she knocked and knocked at the door, but there was no reply, she grew more concerned. She tried opening the front door, but it was locked. She went through the back way, the kitchen door was wide open she got in. "Madame Zhoux! madame Zhoux, are you in! It's Rosie!" she called. There was no answer, she went to the lounge, she wasn't in there, then she went up the stairs to her bedroom. The cottage was a tiny little cottage, suitable for one. There was only one bedroom, a bathroom, a lounge and a kitchen. When she got into the bedroom, she found madame Zhoux in bed. She wasn't breathing, she found an empty bottle of prescription pills by her bed side, and an empty glass of water. She was dead, Rosie called for an ambulance, at least the phone in the house was still working. The ambulance came, and they called the police and a coroner before they took her body away. Her death was ruled as suicide, despite the fact that she had no motive to take her own life.

It was Roger, Mayor Jenkins, Justin, and John who had killed her. They had gone to her cottage that morning, knocked on her door, and she let them in, only for them to force down her throat the pills. They were angina tablets, that they forced a whole bottle down her throat that she had a massive heart attack. "She can ruin our plans, and we have to take care of her," that is what Roger had told Justin, Mayor Jenkins and John. The four of them worked together. After they forced the pills down her throat, they suffocated her with a plastic bag. Roger took the bag after she was dead, and threw it in the lake by the creek. Rosie cried, and cried, then she went back home to ring Father Thomas to tell him of the news. She also rang Edelbert, and Suzanna to tell them that madame Zhoux was dead. None of them were surprised the least, they were dealing with dangerous people. "I knew something like that was going to happen," said Father Thomas. "Why did you have to drag her into all this? she was a lovely lady" he questioned Rosie over the phone. Rosie was still crying, "I needed help!" she sobbed some more. Since madame Zhoux was a spinister, she had no family, at least no living family, Father Thomas took care of her funeral, at the expense of the church. After the funeral, it wasn't long before Roger was boasting to the villagers that he had bought her house. He removed all her furniture and auctioned it, and he put the cottage up for renting. Rosie was devasted by it all, so was Tobin and Robert. After his brother's death, Father Thomas donated one armed Joe's cottage to charity. It was going to be used as an orphanage. Father Thomas decided to habour the diary and the big black book in the monastery. He took the books to Father Dowling and Father Samuel. He left early Wednesday morning with the books, he felt followed by a beige pick up truck. It followed him all the way to the convent, the minute he turned into the convent drive, the beige pickup drove past. He knew that his life was in danger, but he didn't care. His notion was to save the Lawrence family. He thanked Rosie for letting him see that his brother, one armed Joe was loving, and everything else happened when he was just a boy. Father Thomas arrived at the convent, and was greeted by mother superior. She had no idea of what was going on. He asked to see Father Dowling, and Father Samuel promptly, she went on and called them. "There is a Father Thomas to see you, and he says you know what it is about. Father Dowling and Father Samuel where in the drawing room smoking their pipes and drinking brandy. They hadn't heard the news of madame Zhoux death. The drawing room was a large room, with a large piano on one end, and it was on the second floor of the building. There was a huge crucifix above the fire place, the fire was ablaze. On two walls of the room hosted a library of books, mainly christian books of cause. Behind one wall disguised by the books lay a secret room. "Let him in, and bring him to the drawing room," said Father Samuel over the phone. Sister Margaret who was the mother superior led him to the drawing room. She was dressed in a coronet, and wore a crucifix. The convent was very old fashioned hence the coronets, modern nuns wore veils. She appeared to be in her eighties, and she walked with a walking stick. Her face was haggard, and appeared to be filled with such great sorrow, and emptiness, it was an empathetic face though. She always carried a handkerchief with her because of her constant drooling. She kept wiping her mouth every few minutes, that her handkechief was always wet. All together there was twenty two nuns in the convent. It was over three hundred years old, whereby they started the convent, and slowly introduced a monestary as well. There was always about five monks, and now was only a couple of priests occupying one corner of the convent, Father Samuel being one and then joined by Father Dowling. They had their own quarters, which comprised of three bedrooms, a little chapel, kitchen, lounge, and a drawing room which was also used as a library. It was a stone building with a lot of history attached to it. "Bring him up," said Father Samuel. Mother superior went on to fetch Father Thomas and she took him to Father Samuels quarters. "It's good to see you again Thomas," said Father Dowling. "God bless you Father," said Father Samuel as he got up from his armchair to greet Father Thomas. "Sit down. I have heard so much about you from Father Dowling. So you are the witch hunter," he jeered. "Care for some brandy?" he asked. "Yes thank you that's great," replied Father Thomas as he sat on one of the armchairs. There was no sofas in the drawing room except armchairs, both Father Samuel, and Father Dowling thought armchairs were always good for the back. "Tell us what has been happening in your village?" asked Father Samuel as he lit his pipe sat by the fire. "All sorts, I feel the Lawrence family is in danger; and I wondered if we can do an exorcism of their cottage. By now you should know about Bramwell cottage. The hauntings have been in that cottage for as far as I can remember. I have got bad memories of it from when I was a child living there," responded Father Thomas. "Father Dowling can vow for that, he had encounters himself, and that is why he had to escape here," added Father Thomas. "Monsignor, he even blessed the house," he told me that, and he was chased out of the house by a fleet of bats coming from some air vent," insisted Father Dowling. "The three of us can perform an exorcism," he exclaimed. They were sipping on their brandy while smoking the pipe. "Very well then, when were you thinking of doing the exorcism," he asked while scratching his bold patch. "I was thinking some point mid week, perhaps Wednesday when Mr Lawrence is at work, and the boys in college. "Very well then Wednesday it will be, and we must be prepared," replied monsignor. "Thank you Father, I shall inform Mrs Lawrence then," said Father Thomas. Briefly they spoke about Father Francis and his ill fate, and how he perished during the exorcism at the Abbey ruins. After that they spoke about various other stuff about the church. Father Thomas left feeling hopeful, he was now more than determined to save the Lawrence family. He arrived back at the village and went straight to Bramwell to inform Rosie about the exorcism they were going to perform subject to Rosie agreeing. She agreed, she informed Tobin and Robert even though they were going to be in college on that day. She informed Dr Edelbert and Suzanna, and Doctor Edelbert and Suzanna were going to be there as well.

That same week Father Samuel fell ill, firstly he contracted a fever, then followed by hallucinations. He developed boils all over his body that he was bed ridden. He started vomiting black slugs, just like Audrey did. His face was unrecognisable, every bit of his face was covered with boils that had lava growing inside, till flies were popping out of his face. At some point his bedroom was covered with flies, that Father Dowling had to flick them out threw the window. In his hallucinations he was seeing men in red hooded robes performing something like a ceremony. He was also seeing images of the devil, and of a woman with head full of serpents. It was the sisters of mercy that were nursing him. Father Dowling grew scared, because he heard of it before from Suzanna's family. Suzanna had told him of Audrey, besides he had seen it happen to Father Francis. He called off the exorcism, and chose to wait till Father Samuel got better., Father Thomas regurlary visited him, and so did Rosie, Suzanna, and Edelbert. As he lay in his sick bed, he never put down his rosary beeds, he kept them closely tightened in his hands. Every morning he received holy communion. Every time Suzanna and Edelbert visited, they felt followed by random people. They would follow them right to the entrance of the convent, then drive past. Rosie never lost hope, she prayed everyday for Father Samuel to get better. Weeks passed and Father Samuel was recovering, thanks to the prayers of Father Dowling who never left his side, and to the prayers of the good nuns. The boils disappeared, while the hallucinations remained. One point when Rosie, Edelbert, and Suzanna visited him, he couldn't recognise them. He called Rosie the devil's daughter. They had arrived early morning, and Father Samuel had just woken up. They brought him fruit, and some apple pie. He threw the fruit and apple pie across the room. "I will not accept gifts from the devil's daughter!" he shouted. He was restless, he got out of bed, and started pacing up and down the room. His mobility had become so bad that he was using a walking stick. He threw the walking stick at Rosie. "Get out of my house, you daughter of the devil," he shouted. It was Father Dowling who managed to calm him down. He was so confuesd on that day. He refused all his meals, and was trying to escape from the convent. Father Samuel had living relatives, a brother and sister and nieces and nephews. They too visited him regurlary after they learnt of his ill health.

Back in the village Isabella was being frowned upon by the villagers for moving into the Menderaz's home. She replaced Aida. She wasn't ashamed at all, she felt she had an important role to fulfill in the cult. The wedding was being planned and she held a special place in the cult, organising the wedding. Roger, Mayor Jenkins, Justin, and John were planning a secret ceremonial wedding for

Trevor and Rebecca, it had everything to do with the cult. They didn't inform Rosie for fear that she might spoil the plan for them. It was a Monday full moon when the wedding was going to take place at the Abbey ruins, midnight during the devil's hour. Rosie knew there was going to be a wedding but she wasn't informed on when it was going to take place. Rebecca and Trevor were also unaware of the wedding plan. The Monday of the full moon arrived, it was in the evening that Roger, and Justin paid a visit to Trevor and Rebecca. They were having alcoholic drinks by the balcony, that is when Roger spiked their drinks with some sleeping pills. They woke up at the Abbey ruins wearing wedding attire. Rebecca was in a wedding gown that was red in colour, and she wore a red veil, while Trevor was in a three piece suit that was black in colour, he wore a black shirt and tie as well. They woke up surrounded by a large crowd wearing red clocks with hoods. They were chanting and singing in some weird language. They danced around them throwing some form of fresh herbs on them. Rebecca and Trevor were still drowsy, Roger forced them to drink some potion from a goblet inscribed SAC. The potion tasted vile, but they had very little energy to resist the drink, and they both passed out. When they passed out, Mayor Jenkins surfaced as the cult leader, he stood in the middle of the alter, and started reading from some book, while the rest chanted and danced around Trevor and Rebecca. They tied them up on torture stakes, that is when John appeared with the silver dagger inscribed SAC. Rebecca and Trevor were in the middle of the the alter, right in the centre of the hexagram. John had been rehearsing his role, guided by Roger, and Mayor Jenkins. He lifted the silver dagger up, and read something from a book, the rest of them were still chanting. He moved towards Trevor and stabbed him in the heart. Isabella was the only woman there, she was holding a chalice, of which she filled with Trevor's blood. She passed the chalice to Mayor Jenkins, who drank from it; he then passed it on to Justin and Justin drank from it as well. From there he passed it to John, and John followed suit, then they passed to everybody there. They all drank Trevor's blood. He died on the cross without even knowing it. Next Mayor Jenkins moved on to Rebecca, he asked John to stab her in the heart with the dagger, and drink from her blood first. John agreed. He stabbed his own daughter and drank her blood, before passing the chalice to Mayor Jenkins and the rest of the cult members. As prophesied in the big black book, Rebecca was twenty three, and had dark hair that is why she fitted the part of the she godess. As Rebecca and Trevor were dying on the torture stake, the ground shook in the village, that even Rosie and her boys felt it. They woke up, and gathered in the drawing room. There was mourning sounds coming from the walls, and blood was dripping out of the walls. Bells were ringing in the cottage, and they heard chanting noises in the cottage. The chantings carried on through out the whole night. By now Rosie and the boys were used to escapedes happening in their cottage. After Rebecca and Trevor died, they burnt their bodies in a born fire while they danced around and summoning the she godess. A huge green serpent appeared in the fire and was hissing away, before it disappeared when the fire went out. "Our lord is going to return!" they chanted away. After that Isabella was pronounced as the new priestess of the cult. Rosie and the boys had another sleepless night. John came back at dawn, because him, Roger, Mayor Jenkins, and Justin had to clear up the Abbey, and tie up any loose ends. The minute he walked in, the chantings stopped. "Where have you been?" asked Rosie. "I was with Justin just making plans for the wedding," he replied. "I am awefully tired, I will speak to you later," he said then went straight to bed. The blood on the walls simply vanished, as if it was never there.

 Days that followed Rosie was struggling to get hold of Rebecca, she tried telephoning her, but there was no reply. She went to her place several times and knocked on the door, but there was no answer. That is when she grew suspicious, she told John, but John was dismissive. "Call the police if you are worried," he said. The head of the police in the village was called George, and he was also a member of the cult. Rosie went to the police station, but the policemen were reluctant to help. She contacted Edelbert and Suzanna, and told them of Rebecca's disappearance. From hearing that, Edelbert and Suzanna knew that Rebecca and Trevor had been sacrificed as written in the black book. However they chose not to tell Rosie. She got the boys to enquire from Charles, but Charles hadn't heard from Trevor neither. He was worried about his brother as well. He also had gone to Trevor and Rebecca's house but they were not in." The wedding is just round the corner, how can we organise anything if they are not there!" cried Rosie as she spoke to Justin over the phone. "I'm sure they are okay and they will show up," replied Justin. "Don't you worry now my dear, why don't you relax that pretty head of yours, and leave that with me and John," he smirked. As days passed, Roger sold Ms Biggs house to a middle aged couple from the village, and he pocketed the money. Rosie didn't know anything about it, till she went knocking on the door looking for Rebecca. To her surprise she was greeted by some strangers who claimed they had purchased the house from Roger. Rosie had no choice but to put the wedding plans to a hault, instead she had to find Rebecca and Trevor since nobody else in the village cared to do so. Days passed and weeks passed, Rosie and the boys were still searching for Rebecca and Trevor, but to no avail. Her last resort was to push Father Thomas for the exorcism of Bramwell, by then Father Samuel was fully recovered. His hallucinations disappeared the minute Rebecca and Trevor died on the torture stake. Rosie didn't feel stalked anymore by strangers, and was the same for Edelbert, Suzanna, and Father Thomas. The cult had achieved what they set out to achieve, and that is to pave the way for the second coming of Father Santos through a virgin sacrifice coming from Bramwell. By that time Rosie's marriage to John had become so estranged that they were not even sleeping in the same bed, he was sleeping in Rebecca's old room instead. They hardly spoke, and he was the same towards Tobin and Robert. In the mean time Isabella was well established in the Menderaz's household. Rosie tried finding Aida but without success. According to Justin she had moved back with her parents, but Rosie had gotten their address from Charles, but they hadn't heard from her. 'Did he kill Aida?' Rosie thought to herself. She was now suspicious of Justin. 'Justin, Roger, and Mayor Jenkins probably killed Aida, so as to pave way for Isabella,' thought Rosie.

Chapter 12

Rosie, Edelbert, Suzanna; alongside Father Thomas, Father Dowling, and Father Samuel agreed on performing the exorcism, and the day was on a Wednesday when none of them had other commitments. Tobin and Robert were also to partake, meaning that they had to be out of college that day, that was the agreement. Suzanna was beginning to have cold feet, she didn't want to relive the experience that she did with her family, it was too painful, so she decided not to partake. She convinced Edelbert not to neither. "They are in the good hands of the priests, and they shall be fine," she uttered to Edelbert. Edelbert did not argue with her neither, he was scared for his life. "You don't want to die there neither, and you are the last of your family to be alive," responded Edelbert. "It makes sense that we do not partake, after all what can we do there, absolutely nothing, except be by-standers," exclaimed Edelbert. John was going to be out working, that is why it was important to perform the exorcism in the morning. Rosie was excited and at the same time scared that the entity could kill them, the whole lot of them like it did with Suzanna's family. "Are you sure this is going to work," she asked the Monsignor over the phone. "I can't guarantee anything Mrs L. I have never performed an exorcism before, we are all risking our lives here. It can only go either way, do you understand? Are you sure you want to follow this path? You have got a couple of days to think about it," stated the Monsignor. Rosie had given it a good thought, and she was determined to have the exorcism done, she wanted to save Rebecca. She thought the cult had hidden Rebecca and Trevor somewhere, and that John knew of their whereabouts. The cult members were restless, waiting for something, something important was coming up. Somehow they knew that Rosie was planning on some exorcism.

Wednesday morning, all the cult members gathered at the Abbey ruins, they held a meeting. While they were having their meeting Father Thomas, Father Dowling, and Father Samuel were already at Bramwell. The boys were up, they knew of what was going to happen, and Father Samuel was putting them, and Rosie in place. 'I wish madame Zhoux was here,' thought Rosie. Edelbert had rung Rosie and informed her that he and Suzanna were not going to make it. He had left her with words of encouragement. Father Samuel started off by blessing the house with holy water, nothing unusual happened. "Let's us start," he said. The exorcism was to take place in Rebecca's room. He got his gear ready, the three priests had their exorcism bibles, and holy bibles. They started off with the Lord's prayer, then Father Samuel started reading from the exorcism bible, a gush of wind swept through the room. Immedietely there was blood on the walls, before Father Samuel got tossed by an unseen force to the other end of the room. Next to be tossed in the air was Father Thomas, then Father Dowling. They started hearing chantings coming from the walls, church bells, and whistling sounds. "Remain strong!" yelled father Samuel. He got up, and carried on reading from the exorcism bible. A swam of bats came flying out of the air vent, followed by flies. They covered the whole room. "They are not real! remain focused! yelled Father Samuel. The cult members had left the Abbey ruins and now surrounded Bramwell, John was there as well. They had carried twigs and firewood with them, and a few had cans of kerosene. John let them in the cottage, they poured kerosene all over the ground floor and lit a match. Bramwell went in flames, and the priests, Rosie, and the boys couldn't get out, til they all perished in the cottage. Word got round to Suzanna and Edelbert who were waiting in anticipation. They were glad that they had backed down from attending the exorcism. The villagers danced round Bramwell as it burnt down, with Mayor Jenkins in charge. After the fires went out, Mayor Jenkins, Justin and Roger grabbed John, tied him up and through him inside the cottage. The villagers poured kerosene on him and watched him burn to death. While he was burning, they danced around chanting," It is done!" repeatedly. Mayor Jenkins, Roger and Justin all shook hands, and smiled joyfully.

After all that, days went back to normal in the village, Isabella was now well established in the Mendereraz' household. Nobody knew whatever happened to Aida, and Mayor Jenkins ordered the rebuilding of Bramwell. It took them a year to rebuild Bramwell, and of cause they were waiting for the next family to move in there. As for Suzanna, she moved back with auntie Doris, and Edelbert went back to his old hospital routine.